UDDER NONSENSE

More Tales from Frost Heaves

Fred Marple

For Dad, who told the
very first story.

Disclaimer

In my last book, I made some comments that a few folks from town took exception to. I won't say which folks or which comments or we'd be here all day. But after that, the other folks on the FRED council decided they'd better cover themselves. So they asked me to include the following paragraph right up front.

> *The views and opinions expressed by Fred Marple do not necessarily reflect those of the town of Frost Heaves, the Frost Heaves Regional Economic Development council, or the citizens of Frost Heaves including, but not limited to, his wife, his neighbors, his friends, or even himself, since he doesn't know what he's talking about most of the time and won't remember it five minutes later anyway.*

Introduction

My name is Fred Marple and I represent FRED, the Frost Heaves Regional Economic Development council. As I explained in my first book, our goal has been to put the town of Frost Heaves, New Hampshire, back on the map, maybe bring in some progress and get people to pay more attention to us. (I'm sorry if I'm repeating myself, but we may have some newcomers and I don't want 'em to get any more confused than they already are.)

The response to that first book was so great—several folks said they stayed awake all the way to the end—that I decided to write another one. I wanted this one to be a bestseller, so I planned to make it a racy book, like *Peyton Place*. The problem is, folks in Frost Heaves never really get up to anything very interesting, let alone scandalous. Even our vices tend to be humdrum. So racy was out, mostly.

This time out, I have organized the stories by season, starting with summer. That's our favorite season, not to mention the shortest; last year, summer was on July 17 from about 2:30 to 4 p.m. But I have pretty much given equal time to all the seasons just to show that I don't hold a grudge, despite the killer icicle that tried to take me out last winter.

TABLE OF CONTENTS

SUMMER

Duck, Duck, Goof

The guys from the Loon Lodge held a fundraiser last weekend. I've told you about the Loon Lodge, it's a gaggle of old guys who hang out at the lodge at Lake Mahoosic. They have a motto, based loosely on the Marine Corps motto "Semper Fidelis," which is Latin for "Always Faithful." The Loon Lodge Motto is "Semper Aliquid," which is Latin for "It's Always Something." That's fitting in a couple of ways, because whenever these guys get together, there is always a liquid involved— usually beer—and something is bound to go wrong.

For a while now, the guys had been wanting to buy one of them flat-screen TVs for the lodge so they could watch Big Time Wrestling or Big Time Bowling or whatever. (Basically, they will watch anything that starts with the words "Big Time," including Big Time Lawn Mowing and Big Time Napping.) But those TVs cost a bit, and what with repairs to the lodge roof and the annual Beef Jerky festival, the available cash in the Loon Lodge kitty is about what you'd find if you did a good search between your sofa cushions.

The lodge members kicked around a few ideas, discarded several—including a raffle for Arthur Bascom's matchbook collection and a cookbook with 101 ways to use zucchini—and settled on one of them duck race events, where you pay for a plastic duck with a number on it and all the ducks are put in a stream and the person whose duck crosses the finish line first gets a prize.

Let's just say, this didn't work out so well. To begin with, Bert Woodbury suggested it would be more interesting if they used real ducks instead of plastic ones. The rest of the guys, displaying their usual lack of foresight, said, "Why not?"

They borrowed a few dozen White Pekin ducks from Homer Andrews, and right away they ran into trouble. To begin with, putting a number on a live duck turned out to be harder than they expected, a lot more complicated than a plastic duck. Let's just say the ducks weren't all that interested in participating in the fundraiser.

Eventually though, after a lot of squawking and feathers flying, the guys did manage to get the ducks numbered using water-based paint and a thin brush. On the day of the race, they loaded the fowl into the back of Walter Dunton's van and took them to Miller's brook at the edge of town, which runs down into the town pond. By now, what with the indignity of being numbered—it turns out that Pekin ducks take a lot of pride in their pure white coats—and being jostled around in the back of Walter's van, the birds were even less thrilled to be participating in this event, bordering on irritated, and a few were righteously outraged.

So when Bert and Walter opened the back door of the van, the ducks took off in a storm of protest. It hadn't occurred to them that they'd need more men, they were relying a little too much on the old "like a duck to water" adage. They tried to shoo the reluctant poultry into the brook, but that only drove them down the road towards town.

In town, the other members of the lodge and the ticket holders were gathered by the pond where the brook flows in, waiting to see which duck would cross the finish line first. Needless to say, they were surprised to hear quacking coming down the street and turned to see the ducks parading down Main Street as if this was some kind of special event being put on just for them.

One of the ducks veered off and took a shortcut through Agnes Letourneau's backyard. Agnes is a senior citizen and she has been having a hard time making ends meet lately, what with the price of food going up all the time. She keeps a line of plaster saints on top of her piano and she had been petitioning Saint Elizabeth for a little help with the grocery bill, but so far, Liz hadn't pulled through for her.

That particular day, Agnes was sitting at the kitchen table looking over her grocery list when she heard a chuckling sound coming from the backyard. She looked out the back door and saw a duck nibbling at the bird seed under her feeder. The duck had a number 12 painted on its side and it just happens that Agnes lives at 12 Main Street, so she knew right away that this bird was a special delivery from God to her, though she wasn't sure whether to credit Saint Elizabeth or Saint Francis, the patron saint of animals, who stood right next to Elizabeth on the piano and might have been eavesdropping.

At any rate, Agnes was not someone to look a gift duck in the mouth, or beak as it were. Let's just say that that duck was removed from the competition pretty quick.

That same morning, Alfred Cooper was getting ready to check on his entry in the Most Beautiful Woodpile contest, which we hold annually. Alfred had won the contest every year for as long as we can remember. He is obsessive about his woodpile. For him, it's not just a pile, it's a work of art.

Alfred builds his woodpile on a hill up behind his house where it gets the perfect amount of sun and air circulation. This is not your average woodpile, this is a 5-star wood palace, and before gaining admission, every log has to meet strict guidelines for length, shape, and quality. And it is top-notch construction. Nothing is going to make Alfred's woodpile fall over short of a direct nuclear strike.

This year, Alfred decided to go all out. He made his woodpile into a log cabin, complete with an arched doorway, windows with potted plants in them, and a walkway with cornstalks and pumpkins leading up to it. It was a masterpiece, the Taj Mahal of woodpiles.

In contrast, there was Jenny McDonald's woodpile. Jenny rents the house next to Alfred and she is a single mom, so she don't have time to spend stacking wood neatly. Truth to tell, she don't have time to talk on the phone, take a shower, or read anything longer than a permission slip for her kid's field trip to the pumpkin farm. She rarely has a chance to hold a conversation that doesn't involve an argument about cutting Barbie's hair with the kitchen shears.

As a result, Jenny's woodpile has more of a natural look, only slightly tidier than your average beaver dam. She does keep the woodpile covered, but half the time the tarp is blowing off, providing the wood with about as much protection from the elements as a Fredericks of Hollywood negligée. There is generally a community of wild things living in Jenny's woodpile, like a critter condo with chipmunks, snakes, skunks, spiders, and other creatures occupying various sections.

The state of Jenny's woodpile never bothered her, but it drove her neighbor Alfred crazy. Every time he looked over at her backyard and saw that jumbled mess, his skin began to itch.

One evening, he just couldn't stand it anymore. Jenny waitresses in the evenings at the Bluebell Diner while her daughter goes to her mom's house, so there wasn't anyone around. Alfred snuck over to Jenny's woodpile to do a little tidying up. He surprised a couple of garter snakes who did not appreciate the renovation, but that didn't bother him.

The problem was that Alfred is not the kind of guy who can leave a job half done. The next evening, he saw how bad the rest of Jenny's pile looked compared to the part he had neatened up, so he went over and did some more.

This went on for a few days, and of course, Jenny never noticed, because as I say, she don't have a lot of time to be staring out the window at her woodpile. But that woodpile was looking better and better.

Finally, the Saturday came for the judging of the Most Beautiful Woodpile contest. Alfred had been away on

Friday and had gotten home late, so he hadn't had a chance to do the usual last-minute touchups to his pile.

He got up in the morning, stepped out the back door and heard what sounded like a bunch of old ladies cackling. He stopped and listened, and then he recognized the sound: ducks.

He ran for the woodpile, and even from a distance, he could see that it was a mess: duck droppings everywhere, plants all knocked over, and loose logs scattered about.

Alfred let loose a trumpet blast of profanity and ran to the pile just as a big old duck with a number 1 painted on his side appeared in the doorway of the log cabin.

"Shoo," Alfred yelled, but that old duck just stared at him, as if the two of them were standing at opposite ends of a western street getting ready for the big showdown. The other ducks got real quiet, just like in the movies. You could almost hear the theme from "The Good, The Bad and The Ugly" whistling in the wind.

What Alfred didn't know was that this duck's name was Rufus. He was the alpha duck from Homer Andrews' farm and he had a reputation for being mean, cantankerous, and just generally nasty. Rufus had been raised with geese who picked on him, and as a result, he grew up to be a pretty tough bird himself. Over the years, he'd had many confrontations with postal workers, delivery people, census workers, and other visitors to the farm. He may have been the only duck in New Hampshire with a rap sheet.

Alfred took a step towards the doorway. "Shoo!"

Rufus started to make a noise, a low rumble that surprised Alfred because he didn't know that ducks could growl.

Alfred picked up one of the logs that had been knocked down and moved a little closer. Rufus put his wings up to let Alfred know he weren't going to be intimidated.

The next few minutes were a bit fuzzy for Alfred. There was a lot of squawking and shouting—including more expletives that I will not repeat here—and wings flapping, and logs being knocked loose. In the end, Rufus and the other ducks decided their new home wasn't in such a good neighborhood after all and decided to move on. As they squawked away, Alfred stood there breathing hard, surveying his once-beautiful woodpile and shaking his head.

Just then, he heard a car pull into his driveway and turned around to see Herb Cullen and the other judges from the Most Beautiful Woodpile contest getting out of the car. They all looked kind of confused at Alfred's devastated pile, but they were reserving judgment because this was Alfred Cooper, perennial winner of the woodpile contest. They figured maybe he had gone in an entirely different direction. Maybe this pile was supposed to be like modern art, some statement about the impermanence of human achievement as manifested by nature's gradual destruction.

But folks in Frost Heaves are not modern art aficionados, so Alfred did not win this year. In the end, the winner of the Most Beautiful Woodpile contest was a surprise, a sleeper entry. The judges gave first prize to Jenny McDonald, whose woodpile was also honored as the Most Improved. Jenny was thrilled to get the Golden Stump trophy and the $50 gift certificate to the Bait and Beauty Salon.

As far as the duck race goes, the winner was Cliff Beaman, who works at the town garage. Cliff's was the only duck to actually cross the finish line at the town pond. Of course, a lot of people cried fowl. (Sorry, it had to be done.) Among the many losers was Homer Andrews, who was out two ducks—one that ended up in Agnes' freezer and another one that ran off with a wild turkey—that's a story for another day.

After the various expenses, including replacing those missing ducks, the guys at the Loon Lodge cleared $13.41, which was not enough to buy a flat screen TV. It was, however, enough to buy one of them 3-D View-Masters and some reels of Hawaiian hula dancers, so the guys were happy enough. At least the View-Master was something they could set up, no matter how much they had drunk, which probably wouldn't have been true about the flat-screen TV.

NEWS NUGGETS:
Dance Classes Offered

Rhonda LaFleur from the Bait and Beauty salon is teaching a new exercise class up to the high school, Rhumba with Rhonda. Basically, it's folks shaking things that were never meant to be shaken, at least not in this neck of the woods or by people of this age. Right now, the attendees are mostly women, but Rhonda says men are welcome to attend, so the odds are pretty good. Of course, the goods are pretty odd.

Swap Shop Justice

There has been a kerfuffle lately at the town dump, or more specifically, at the swap shop at the dump, the place where slightly and not-so-slightly used stuff goes to find a new home. The swap shop is the Filene's Basement of Frost Heaves, the center of local commerce.

Louise Mitchell is head of the swap shop committee, a group of ladies who take care of the shop. They call themselves the "Dumplings," although Louise likes to think of herself as a "docent." That's a fancy French word that means "person who makes sure you ain't dropping off junk and picking up stuff just to sell on eBay."

Being the chief guardian of the goods means Louise gets first dibs on the stuff that comes into the shop, a fact that bothers some folks, though most people don't seem to mind. This is not Sotheby's, after all. We are not talking heirloom antiques here.

Of course, there's no telling what some folks put stock in, and therein lies the problem. It all started when Bertha Eldridge asked Louise to keep an eye out for glass vases. Bertha had come up with a new craft for the Snowflake Fair, something to do with paint and fabric.

Anyway, she asked Louise to let her know if any vases came in.

This is a service Louise provides for folks in town, and she has a number of regular subscribers. For example, there's Ellie Beech, who teaches kindergarten at Frost Heaves Elementary School. Ellie is always on the lookout for craft supplies, so if someone drops off a bag of yarn or felt scraps, Louise lets her know right away. She passes along old coffee mugs to Janice at the market because people are forever breaking the mugs there. Then there's an artist fellow who lives back in the woods, he's been collecting old antennas for years. We don't know what he's planning to do with 'em, something arty, I suppose.

When an item comes in that might interest one of Louise's regular customers, she sets it aside and lets them know. It's a pretty good system, or at least it was until the vase incident.

The way it happened was this. Elwood Peabody, who owns the Peabody Inn in town, stopped by the dump to see what he could find. Elwood uses the swap shop as his main source for decorating the inn—lamps, pitchers, side tables. Elwood has never been known to bring anything to the swap shop, which wouldn't surprise you if you knew him, as he comes from a long line of cheapskates. By the time a Peabody is finished with an item, it's not fit for much but the wood stove or the trash bin.

At any rate, Elwood was perusing the items on offer at the swap shop when he happened to see a glass vase that Louise had tucked on the shelf behind the checkout counter, where she keeps things she's holding for people.

"I'll take that vase," Elwood said.

"Oh, I'm holding that for Bertha," Louise said.

Elwood looked around. "Where is she?"

"She's coming in."

"Well, I'm right here."

"I know," Louise said, "but I already let her know I was holding it for her."

"What kind of outfit are you running?" Elwood said. "Is this a town facility or not?"

"Yes, but—"

"You giving special treatment to your friends? Is that what this is?"

Needless to say, this was not the right approach to take with the person in charge of the swap shop if you want to get in on the good stuff. Louise let Elwood know in no uncertain terms that she was holding the vase for Bertha and he could like it or not, as he chose.

I should mention that there was nothing special about this vase, it was the kind you get with the $5.99 bouquet at your average florist, the kind you find by the dozens at yard sales. But Elwood was fit to be tied. You'd think that vase was handmade Tiffany glass, the way he went on.

Elwood decided he wasn't going to take this lying down, so he headed up to the town hall to talk to Edith Wyer, our town clerk. Technically, it was not up to Edith to do anything about this issue, but everybody around here knows if you want to get something done, you've got to get Edith on your side.

Edith wasn't in a particularly good mood that day because she was entering dog licenses into the new computer system and the software was giving her a hard time. There was no category for most of the dogs in Frost Heaves, which is no particular breed at all. A dog that would be considered a mutt in other towns would practically be a purebred in Frost Heaves.

So when Elwood came in to complain about Louise holding things for people at the swap shop, Edith gave him a long answer that essentially boiled down to, "So what?"

"Well," he said, "she shouldn't be able to pick through the junk for friends while being paid by the town."

Edith looked at him over the tops of her glasses. "She isn't being paid. She's a volunteer."

"Well, that doesn't matter. It isn't right. Some of that stuff could be valuable."

"Have you been to our swap shop?" By which she meant that Frost Heaves is not a town like Upper Crustwich, Connecticut or Newbucks, Vermont, where rich people are known to cast off their unwanted valuables.

But Elwood was not giving up that easily. "We need rules. Rules that spell out when you can pick, who can pick, how much you can pick."

Needless to say, Edith was not thrilled about having another set of rules to deal with on top of everything else. She took a deep breath. "All right. Leave it to me. I'll take care of it."

When Edith says she'll take care of something, you know she will, even if you don't know how and you're not sure you *want* to know. It's kind of like The Godfather.

Elwood headed back to the inn, where he was waiting for his bartender Darlene, who was late. Darlene is a single mom and she sometimes has trouble finding someone to look after her son Jason while she's working.

Eventually, the phone rang and it was Darlene. She told Elwood she had picked up Jason at school and was going to drop him off at her mother's house on the way to work, but her car started making an awful screeching sound. She took it to Bundy's garage and Bundy told her he'd look at it, but now she needed a ride to work, and that's why she was calling. Elwood wasn't happy about it, but he needed a bartender, so he went to Bundy's to pick her up.

Darlene and Jason were hanging out in Bundy's waiting area, which has all the warmth and charm of a meat locker. Jason didn't mind this at all, he's a real boy. He loves the cars, the banging, the smell of grease. Plus, Bundy has a great old tonic machine (or, as people from away call it, "soda.") The machine was put in by the Sasagi Beverage Company back when Bundy's dad owned the place. "Sasagi" is an old Abenaki Indian word that means "right" or "just," and the Sasagi Beverage Company has been around since Calvin Coolidge was president.

That old machine is a classic. It's the kind where you put your money in and pull out a bottle, and another one rattles down the pike to take its place. Back in the day, you could get tonic for a nickel, and here's the great thing about that machine. It still takes nickels, and it *only* takes buffalo nickels. No one knows why, but nothing else will work in it. Bundy keeps a supply of buffalo nickels in his cash drawer and if you want a tonic, you give him a dollar and he gives you a nickel for the machine.

Anyway, Jason was happy enough to sit in the waiting area, drinking a Sasagi Cola and watching Bundy go about his work.

When Elwood arrived to pick Darlene up, she said, "Can we drop Jason off at my mother's on the way?"

Elwood didn't really want to, but he figured he didn't have a choice. "All right, come on."

Jason was still holding his tonic bottle as he got into the back seat of Elwood's car. Elwood gave him the hairy eyeball and said, "Don't you dare spill soda on the seat."

Jason just nodded and didn't say a word. He's a little scared of Elwood.

Later that afternoon, Bundy called Darlene at the tavern and told her it was not good news—she was going to need a complete brake job all around. She started crying because the last thing she needed was a bill for new brakes just then, especially given what Elwood was paying her.

"Don't worry about it," Bundy said. "We'll figure something out."

When she got off the phone, Darlene told Elwood about it, but he was not sympathetic. He has no idea what it's like being a single mom these days, and he was thinking some uncharitable thoughts about her financial abilities.

A little while later, Edith called Elwood from the town office. "All right, I took care of things," she said. "That vase is yours if you want to go pick it up."

Elwood was pretty pleased with himself, and he headed right over to the swap shop to pick up his prize. As he was driving, he came to a stop sign—well, *the* stop sign, the only one in the town of Frost Heaves—and the car made a kind of rumbling sound, followed by a loud clunk.

Elwood ignored the noise because he was so happy about getting the better of Louise Mitchell. He strode into the swap shop as if he owned it and Louise handed over the vase, but she didn't say a word. She was none too pleased about his going over her head to Edith Wyer.

Elwood didn't say anything either, but he could tell that the shelf behind Louise had been cleared off. For once, it seemed, justice had been done. He had single-handedly brought about a change of policy at the swap shop, and he was pretty pleased with himself. There was a smirk on his face as he left.

As Elwood drove back to the inn, the car made that clunking noise again, so he called up Bundy to see if he could take a look at it.

"I've got to finish working on Darlene's car," Bundy said. "But I'll get to it after that."

"If that girl would save her money, maybe she could afford something better than that old junk," Elwood said.

"If you paid her a living wage, maybe she could," Bundy said, and hung up.

Later that afternoon, Bundy finished the work on Darlene's car and brought it to the inn for her. He had done his best, but the bill still came to $200. He handed the keys to her and said, "Don't worry about this. Pay me when you can."

Then he took Elwood's car back to the garage, and sure enough, it rumbled and clunked at the stop sign or any time he slowed down quick, just like it had for Elwood. Bundy put the car up on the lift and checked the brakes and all the tires, but there was nothing wrong that he could see. Then, as he was lowering the lift, the car made the sound again, which didn't make any sense.

He poked around inside the car, and that's when he noticed a tonic bottle on the floor behind the passenger's seat. It was a Sasagi Cola bottle, one of his own, and he realized what had happened. Jason had left it on the floor and every time the car came to a stop, the bottle would roll under the seat and hit the seat adjustment at the front and make that clunking sound.

Bundy waited a couple of hours before he called Elwood. "Well, it took a while," he said. "But I fixed it."

"What was the matter?"

"Brakes," Bundy said. "Gonna run you $200, and that's the bargain price."

Elwood fumed for a while, but Bundy wouldn't budge. When Elwood stopped grumbling, Bundy told him to put Darlene on the phone.

"Your bill has been taken care of," he told her.

"By who?"

"A little angel," Bundy said. "Someone very close to you. But you can't say anything to anyone about it."

So that explains the new policy at the swap shop. Louise still saves things for people, but now she puts them under the counter where no one can see them. If you ask her to hold something for you, she hides it there, and you have to give her the secret password, which everyone in town knows, except for Elwood Peabody.

Sasagi.

Police Log:
Where There's Smoke

On Tuesday, police and fire responded to the Bait 'n Beauty salon where Vera Hadley's hair had started smoking. "It's her own fault," said Rhonda LaFleur, owner of the salon. Vera had come in for a dye job and neglected to tell Rhonda she had been dying her own hair at home. "Those cheap store-bought dyes have chemicals that react with professional dyes, which is what caused the smoke," said Rhonda.

Panicky customers called the fire department, but Rhonda had the situation in hand by the time they arrived. According to fire chief Mickey Edwards, "We plan to call on Rhonda if we have any more perm pyrotechnics." He also noted that Vera's hair looked "hot."

101 Ways (More or Less) to Kill a Mosquito

Life in New England is generally good, with only a few things to spoil our overall 5-star rating. (I'm talking New England in general. Ratings for Frost Heaves itself tend to fall in the "OK" to "Needs Improvement" range.)

One of the big drawbacks to life around here is mosquitoes. In some places, killing mosquitoes is just a fact of life. But in Frost Heaves, it's a competition sport. True, there are folks who live in the area for years without ever picking up the finer points of the sport, but that's something they're understandably embarrassed about, like not being able to drive a stick-shift or harboring a secret desire to tear those little tags off of pillows.

In case you're ever planning a summertime visit to Frost Heaves, and as a refresher to those locals who should know better, I thought I'd provide some tips on the fine art of mosquito-killing.

The One-Handed Body Slap

This is the basic mosquito-killing maneuver, which you execute (pun absolutely intended) when you feel the mosquito begin to bite, or you actually see it land on your skin.

Experienced swatters know that mosquitoes are born with hand-evasion radar. It's nearly impossible to sneak up on a mosquito until it finishes sharpening its needle and sticking it into your epithelium (a Greek word that means "over the thelium," which just goes to show that, as smart as they were, the Greeks didn't know everything, since I've been bitten just about everywhere *but* my thelium, although to be honest, I'm not sure where it's located.)

At any rate, championship technique calls for smashing the mosquito after it sticks you but before it actually draws blood. Killing the bug after it has a taste of your vital fluids is unsportsmanlike, not to mention messy. Timing is important here, and there's an element of risk involved that makes the One-Handed Body Slap similar to the more difficult "Make My Day" slap below.

The Two-Handed Slap

This is the first of your fancier, competition slaps. Officially, it's known as the "Two-Handed, Mid-Air Mash," and it's quite a bit more complicated than the basic body slap, since you have to take into account your distance from the bug, the wind speed, and the mosquito's trajectory, velocity, and acceleration. The two-handed slap is a pre-emptive move, performed before the mosquito has even landed on the playing field. As such, this slap bothers some bleeding hearts (and arms, and necks) who think it's unfair, since the mosquito hasn't bitten you yet. But people with more sense know that any mosquito, given the chance, will bite. It's a matter of time.

(By the by, I don't have the space to go into all the theological issues about mosquitoes, such as "Why did God create them in the first place?" If you ask a pastor type, you'll probably get one of two answers:

1. "To provide food for the birds."

This is hogwash, since God came up with plenty of other things for birds to eat, and I can't remember the last time I was bitten by a worm, a sunflower seed, or a suet ball.

2. "It's a result of original sin."

This idea goes back to Saint Walter of Albany, who thought the mosquito was part of God's punishment on Adam and Eve for eating the apple. Walter also figured that God felt bad about it afterwards and made fireflies as a way of apologizing. Let's get this straight: the only good mosquito is a dead mosquito. Now let's get on with it.)

The two-handed slap is a very popular move in Frost Heaves, which is why the local community theater group, the Frost Heaves Artists Repertory Theatre (FHART—it's important to pronounced the "H") usually schedules its performances during mosquito season; if you get enough people doing the two-handed slap, it almost sounds like applause—a little sporadic, but those actors need all the encouragement they can get. Besides, too much applause would probably just startle them and make them forget their lines even more.

The Make My Day Slap

This move is also known as the "Sacrifice Slap." It's often a desperation move, carried out when you can't get to sleep because there's a mosquito buzzing around the bedroom.

To attempt this slap, the swatter turns on a light, throws back the covers, and stares down at the naked portion of his or her body, waiting for the bug to land, then pulverizes it. This isn't a move for beginners, since there's a fair chance of inflicting bruises on yourself. Also, if you're sleeping with someone else—especially someone who isn't bothered by the bug in question—they might not appreciate the shenanigans. But the satisfaction of a successful slap is usually worth it.

The Up Against the Wall, Little Bugger

Now and then, you'll find a mosquito that refuses to take the bait in the Make My Day slap and just lands on a wall when you turn on the light. Of course, as soon as you turn off the light, they'll start up again. If you had ears like Superman, you could probably hear them giggling at this point.

The only way to deal with this situation is to get out of bed and attack the mosquito where it lands, on the wall. On a hot summer night, this can result in a fair number of little blotches on the wall, which you won't really notice till the next morning. But if you do it right, they'll form a kind of pattern, and from a distance it doesn't look that bad. In fact, this technique was the inspiration for those small, repeated print wallpaper patterns that were so popular a few years ago.

Finally, there are a couple of expert moves that beginners probably shouldn't try without supervision.

The Bestseller Press

This one involves flattening a mosquito between the pages of whatever book you are trying to read as you relax in the hammock, the porch rocker, or the beach chair. The move can be a little messy, but again, the satisfaction is worth it. Note, I don't recommended doing this with library books.

The One-Handed, Mid-Air Grab

This is the most difficult of all moves. Some people have tried to perfect it for years without any luck. It involves all the factors of the two-handed slap, but is performed with only one hand. If, by sheer dumb luck, you ever do manage to catch a mosquito this way, don't get cocky, and whatever you do, *don't get excited and open your hand to examine your kill.* More mosquitoes have been returned to the game by this mistake than by any other. The trick is to shake your fist really hard, so that if the bug is still alive, it'll be dizzy when you open your fist, and you'll get another chance to smoosh it.

While I'm at it, I want to clear up some malarkey that might confuse would-be mosquito mashers. Scientists are full of facts about mosquitoes, most of which are hooey, and none of which will do you any good when you're out in the field.

For example, there's the "Sing, No Sting" theory. This states that only male mosquitoes buzz and only female mosquitoes bite. The idea is that if you hear a mosquito buzzing, you don't have to worry about being bitten. This notion—also known as the "Buzzers Don't Bite" theory—is pure grade-A baloney. First of all, no one has ever been able to tell the sex of a mosquito, and any scientist who says he can has either incredibly good eyesight or a vivid imagination. On the other hand, mosquitoes *can* tell the difference, and they use that knowledge with an enthusiasm that would make a rabbit blush. Even if this theory were true, it wouldn't help at all, since mosquitoes are notorious ventriloquists and they often work in pairs: a male will lurk behind a bedpost buzzing, while his partner sneaks up for a silent snack. Don't be taken in by this scheme.

Another useless bit of information is the Carbon Dioxide Factor. According to this superstition, mosquitoes are attracted to the CO_2 in your breath. The obvious implication is that if you hold your breath, mosquitoes won't bother you. This is fine if you aren't really committed to the concept of breathing. Personally, I have a strong attachment to it.

NEWS NUGGETS:
Summer Theatre

The Frost Heaves Actors Repertory Theatre will present its annual "FHART in the Park" festival at Gilchrist Park this summer, featuring that classic musical Les Misérables. "We're a small group, so we'll be doing a stripped-down version," says Thelma Delmar, who heads up the group. "The original show has dozens of people and all kinds of sets, but we only have six people and two sets. We're calling it 'Less Miserable.'"

Loves Labors Crossed

The annual shed tour was last weekend, sponsored by the Ladies Loon League and featuring some of the town's most historic sheds. Folks bought a ticket that let them wander through their neighbors' outbuildings and then come back to the church vestry for cider and donuts.

Among the featured structures was Alfred Cooper's wood shed, where he smoked his first and last cigarette, an incident that still causes him to turn a little green in the gills. It's also the place where Alfred and Agatha Thurston hid during a game of hide and seek when they were kids, another painful memory for him.

It happened like this. Alfred had decided his pa's shed would be the perfect place to hide, and he asked Agatha if she wanted to hide with him. She pretty quickly agreed. They both figured nobody would think to look in the shed. They also figured they would probably be playing a different game than hide and seek.

Alfred and Agatha ran to the shed without anybody seeing them and pulled the door closed behind them. It was dark inside, only one small window high up on the back wall, which let in just enough light to see your way around.

They listened for a while to see if anyone was coming to find them, both of them pretending they were still playing the same game as the other kids. Agatha and Alfred were both 13 years old and in the ninth grade at the Frost Heaves Academy, where they had been studying biology with Mrs. Howard. What they had in mind, of course, was a kind of extracurricular biology lab, about which they would not be writing a report, needless to say.

A few minutes passed, and it looked as if no one was coming to find them. In fact, it sounded as if the other kids had gone home. So they got down to the real business at hand.

There followed a period of negotiation about who was going to show what to whom during this biology lesson. Alfred was at some disadvantage as he had less on the table, anatomically speaking, and Agatha was a canny negotiator. But they finally came to an agreement and had just started the tedious process of unbuttoning and unfastening when they heard footsteps coming toward the shed, crunching slowly over dry leaves.

They froze, holding their breath, not even daring to rebutton. Agatha was Catholic, a rarity in Frost Heaves, and she knew she had already committed several sins just by being in this place with a boy who was a Protestant. Alfred's concerns were more practical than spiritual. Yes, he was a Protestant, baptized at the Frost Heaves Community Church when he was still in diapers, but the application hadn't really taken hold yet. He did remember something about the lust of the eyes and the lust of the flesh, both of which he had been looking forward to. But right now, he was remembering something Reverend

Giltmore had said during a sermon one Sunday morning: "Be sure, your sin will find you out."

The footsteps grew closer, pausing, then moving, twigs snapping underfoot, and finally stopped just outside the shed door. Then came the sound of snuffling and rooting around, accompanied by an occasional grunt.

Alfred breathed a sigh of relief. "It's just Eloise," he said.

Agatha was still apprehensive. "Who?"

"My pa's sow."

Eloise was his father's favorite pig, matriarch of prizewinning litters. She weighed about 500 pounds and had free rein of the farm during the daylight hours. She also had excellent hearing; she had probably heard someone in the shed and come to investigate.

Alfred went to the door and hissed in a loud whisper, "Eloise! Scat."

At the sound of Alfred's voice, the pig stopped rooting around and grunted inquisitively.

"Go on, git!" Alfred said.

Eloise gave a happy snort. She knew Alfred, had known him since she was just a piglet, and she had always liked him. She grunted again and lay down, plopping her entire quarter-ton weight against the shed door and rocking the whole building.

Alfred glanced at Agatha, who didn't look happy to be stuck in a building with a pig as the world's biggest doorstop. Alfred was remembering that verse from the pastor's sermon, only now instead of sin, it went, "Your swine will find you out."

Alfred gave the door a shove, but there was no moving Eloise's massive bulk. "Eloise, get up."

The pig grumbled contentedly, rearranging her bulk slightly but not moving at all.

"I mean it, pig. Move."

Eloise snorted. She liked the sound of Alfred's voice, it didn't matter what he was saying.

Alfred kneeled at the bottom of the door. "Come on, Eloise," he said, wishing he weren't pleading with a pig in front of Agatha Thurston.

Now Eloise began to snore.

Alfred had had enough. "Look, if you don't get up right now, you are going to be bacon!"

But Eloise's breathing was a deep, contented rumble. She wasn't planning on moving any time soon.

"Dang it." Alfred collapsed, his back against the door.

"Now what?" Agatha asked.

Alfred pondered the situation. Clearly, the biology lesson was over for the day. "Guess we'll just have to wait for supper time when Pa calls her."

Agatha harrumphed, crossed her arms over her chest, and took a seat against the back wall of the shed, far enough away to rule out any further extracurricular activity.

The rumble of Eloise's snoring echoed inside the shed. A fly banged against the back window, trying to get out. From the angle of light coming through the window, they could tell the afternoon sun was starting to set.

Then they heard more footsteps coming toward the shed. These were heavier than Eloise's footsteps, two feet rather than four, and headed right for the shed, where they stopped.

"There you are, pig," Alfred's pa said. "What the dickens you doing here?"

Now Alfred was really worried. At this stage of his spiritual development, he was less concerned with the wrath of God then the wrath of Alfred Cooper, Sr., who was actually, physically present and whose wrath was accompanied by actual, physical ramifications. Alfred Sr. was a deacon at the Frost Heaves Community Church and he took infractions of God's law seriously.

The good news was, Alfred's pa seemed to be talking to Eloise and not to him and Agatha.

"Come on now," Alfred Sr. said to the pig. "Let's go."

Eloise usually listened to Alfred Sr. because he was the keeper of the grain bucket. But now she just raised one complacent eyelid at him, snorted, and went back to sleep.

"Eloise," Alfred Sr. said, "you are the laziest, most shiftless creature the Lord put on this earth, second only to that son of mine. If I've told him once, I've told him a thousand times to clean out your pen. If he don't do it soon, his hide is gonna be more tanned than that saddle of mine. Now, get up."

He made a clucking noise with his tongue, the noise he always made when it was feeding time, and Eloise hoisted herself up. For a pig, she was pretty light on her feet and could run like a racehorse when there was food at the finish line.

Agatha and Alfred heard his father and Eloise heading across the field to the barn and waited until their footsteps faded away. Alfred looked at Agatha, and there was just enough light from the window to see that she was glaring at him. "Guess we better go," he said.

Agatha said nothing but bustled past him, pushed the shed door open, and headed for home.

Alfred decided this might be a good time to muck out Eloise's pen. It wasn't the way he had planned on spending his afternoon, but all things considered, it was probably better than some of the alternatives.

As he shoveled the dirty straw onto the pile behind the barn, he got to thinking about the story of the prodigal son, one of the few lessons he remembered from Sunday school. That guy had been slopping pigs when he decided to come home to his father. The point of the story, as Alfred recalled, was that the father was glad to see his son even though he had messed up so bad. The surprise ending was that the father had forgiven the son—almost as surprising as Alfred's pa not saying anything about him being in the shed with Agatha. Because Alfred was pretty sure his father had known he was in there.

Nowadays, the shed belongs to Alfred Jr., as does the rest of the farm, which he inherited from his pa just after he married Linda Henderson. Alfred's livestock includes a prize sow descended from Eloise. He loves that pig and dotes on her just as much as his pa did Eloise. He named her Agatha.

NEWS NUGGETS:
Sign of the Times

A new highway sign has been installed on Lazybrook Road, thanks to a grant from Homeland Security. The sign reads, "SPEED CHECKED BY RADAR." According to Chief Spaulding, it should cut down on speeding quite a bit. "We don't actually have radar," he notes. "The government only gave us enough for the sign." Still, he figures it might work, given the IQ of the folks who drive that road, though he isn't mentioning any names.

How Everett Beat
the High Cost of Oat Crispies

Everett Northrup stood in the cereal aisle at the Frost Heaves Market and shook his head. I say "aisle" but it's really more of a "section"—your choices at the market tend to be limited.

Everett had stopped by the market to replenish his supply of Oat Crispies cereal, but was aghast to see that the price had risen almost a dollar since the last time he bought it. He checked the other cereals, and they had all gone up as well.

He thought about going elsewhere to get his Oat Crispies, but the options are limited around here. He could drive all the way to the Shop-A-Lot in Fridley, but he hates going to the Shop-A-Lot, which has nineteen checkout stands but never more than two cashiers working at any given time. There is also a "10 Items or less" line, but that always has twenty people standing in it, and if anyone gets to the head of the line in less than half an hour, the store rings a bell and gives them a prize.

Then there are the big warehouse stores like Food Supreme and Grocerama, which remind Everett of converted airplane hangars; by the time he gets to the back of the store, he feels as if he'll have to go through customs to return to the front. They also have those cash registers that print out a long list of what you bought, which Everett destroys as soon as he gets home. He doesn't plan to get in trouble with the law, but if he does, he doesn't want people rummaging through his trash and finding out that he buys Ring-Dings and the Soap Opera Digest.

The only other option for groceries in Frost Heaves is the QwikiMart out on the highway, one of those convenience stores that sells things you're likely to need desperately between the hours of 8 p.m. and midnight and are willing to pay any price for—nacho chips, Velveeta, Heavenly Hash ice cream, and so on. The QwikiMart does carry some regular food like bread and milk, but the prices are even worse than at the market.

While Everett was pondering his options, he studied the ingredients on the Oat Crispies box: rolled oats, sugar, salt, and preservatives. Then he checked out the Wheat Flakes: wheat, sugar, salt, and preservatives. Corn flakes were corn, sugar, salt, and preservatives. He was beginning to see a pattern.

Everett decided he could make his own cereal. He already had sugar and salt at home, so all he needed was rolled oats. He couldn't find rolled oats, so he bought regular oats, figuring he could roll them himself. He also couldn't find any preservatives, but he decided these were going to be all-natural flakes.

When he got home, Everett combined the oats with sugar, salt, and some water into a mixture that looked like organic wallpaper paste. He spread the mixture in a thin layer on a cookie sheet like one big flake. He wasn't sure how to bake it, but decided to try high heat for a short period of time.

Into the oven it went. After about 8 minutes at 450 degrees, Everett's monster flake turned brown and curled up at the edges. It looked like a map of Albania.

Everett had planned to break the megaflake into little pieces, but it wasn't as crispy as he'd expected, and he ended up tearing it into chunks that looked like anemic postage stamps.

Then came the moment of truth. He dumped his homemade flakes into a bowl, poured milk over them, and ladled a triumphant spoonful into his mouth.

"Mmm," he mumbled. "Not bad."

He was lying. His homemade cereal tasted like bits of leather with milk poured over them. If anyone were to sell this, the advertising campaign would be "Leather Crispies—A Tough Cereal for a Tough World."

Nevertheless, Everett ate the whole bowl—he is a Yankee, and we don't waste anything. But he decided to leave cereal making to the flake engineers at Kellogg and General Mills. He did start buying his Oat Crispies at Food Supreme. With a coupon, the price is about what he used to pay for them. I can verify this because he showed me the receipt to prove it. But he did make me promise not to tell anyone what else was on it.

NEWS NUGGETS:
Not that Free

Fire Chief Mickey Edwards reports that he has been remodeling his bathroom. He put the old toilet and sink out on his skimobile trailer with a sign in front that said, "Free." Within a day, the trailer was gone.

"That's bad enough, but they left the toilet and sink behind," says Mickey. If you have Mickey's trailer, please bring it back. Mickey isn't the spiteful sort, but if you ever have a fire at your place and he sees that trailer, let's just say you aren't going to get the best service, if you know what we mean.

Signal Minded

The big news in town is that Frost Heaves has a new radio station, owned and operated by Harvey Delmar. The call letters are WHAT, which stands for "Harvey And Thelma"—Thelma is his wife. He also picked the name because it seemed appropriate in a town where so many folks are hard of hearing. Every time someone says, "What?" Harvey feels like he's getting free advertising for the station.

WHAT is a low-power station, which means that on a windy day it might reach the far side of town. Harvey runs it as a kind of hobby, sitting at his kitchen table, mostly playing his old records, and that makes for an interesting mix. You might hear "Fire and Rain" followed by a John Phillips Sousa march, then "Good Golly, Miss Molly," and after that Patti Page singing "How Much is That Doggie in the Window?" It's kind of a musical trail mix.

When Harvey's not playing music, he airs syndicated educational programs, which he gets for free. It is some scintillating stuff, let me tell you. My favorite is *You and Your Chainsaw*, but my missus is fond of *The Recycling Hour*. Every evening at suppertime, Harvey flips a switch and puts on *The Happy Button Collector* while he and Thelma eat dinner.

But a couple weeks ago, Harvey did something wrong, and instead of *The Happy Button Collector*, what went out over the air was the sound of Harvey and Thelma eating dinner and gossiping about Thelma's cousin Leroy, whose daughter had run off with a porta-potty distributor, which in that family was considered social climbing.

It wasn't until they finished dinner that Harvey realized what had happened and that everyone in town had listened in on their conversation. Well, he panicked. He was sure the FCC was going to shut him down. At the very least, he and Thelma would be the laughing stock of town.

Harvey waited a couple of days for the other shoe to drop, but nothing happened. It turns out the FCC doesn't listen to those low-power stations. Hardly anyone does, except in Frost Heaves, where gossip is the chief form of entertainment. And it seems that more people listened to that evening's broadcast than any other, far more than ever listened to *The Happy Button Collector*.

So now, for the past few weeks, everybody in town has been tuning in to *The Dinner Hour with Harvey and Thelma Delmar*, partly out of self-protection; if people are talking about you, you should probably know what they're saying. Harvey is thinking about going big time and getting national distribution.

Meanwhile, up at the Frost Heaves Community Church, the church board has been wrestling with financial problems. The problem is the church building, which is several hundred years old. Buildings are like people; when you're young, your body seems uncomplicated because everything operates the way it should. You have no idea how intricate and complicated the body is because, for the most part, everything is working smoothly. It's not until you get older and things start to break down that you realize what a complex system it is.

These days, the church building has a lot of things wrong with it, some little and some big, and the church board spends a lot of time figuring out ways to pay for fixes, considering ways to raise money other than hitting up the congregation. The church members are good people, but they are Yankees, and getting them to part with money is like prying barnacles off a boat.

One member of the board, Dave Miller—he is our technology whiz—presented an offer from a cell phone company to put a cell tower inside the church steeple. We do not have good cell phone coverage in Frost Heaves, and this is a matter of grave concern to some folks in town, especially those under the age of 18.

Millie Tuttle was dead set against this idea—she doesn't approve of high technology in the church, or anywhere else, for that matter. And for once, Pastor Woodstead sided with Millie. He wished they could spend less time thinking about money and more time thinking about how to get young people into the church. There are only a few young families in church to begin with, and once the kids become teenagers, they hardly ever darken the door of the church, which is a real concern for him.

Anyway, the board voted to go ahead with the cell tower idea, despite Millie's objections. The cellular company came, took all kinds of measurements, installed the tower inside the steeple, and when they were through, you couldn't even tell it was there.

Most folks in town were excited about this, except for the Millie Tuttle faction, of course. The day the company turned the tower on, a sizeable crowd gathered outside the church, cell phones in hand. The engineer flipped the switch and everyone stared at their little screens, but no one was getting a signal. The engineer scratched his head and went up to the tower to check things, then tried again. This went on for quite a while, but there still wasn't any signal.

It took a while, but the engineer finally figured out the problem. Some time ago, the inside of the church steeple had been lined with copper flashing. Copper is really good at preventing the transmission of electromagnetic waves, including cell phone signals. The transmission signals were coming up from an underground cable to the tower and just bouncing around inside the steeple. It turned out that the only place in town where you could get cell phone reception—excellent reception, in fact—was right below the steeple, inside the church.

The first Sunday after the cell tower was installed, Pastor Woodstead was surprised to see a good turnout for the morning service, better than he'd seen in months. He was especially surprised when the last few rows filled up with young people. He was worried that they might get a little rowdy, but they weren't fooling around. They just sat quietly, staring down at their Bibles and hymnbooks.

After a while, of course, he realized that they were really staring at their cell phones, and text messaging their friends and surfing the web. But he didn't say anything.

He figured that as long as they were in church, they might pick up something of value.

As it happens, the hymn for that morning was "God Moves in a Mysterious Way," which is certainly true. Sometimes the biggest disasters turn out to be the very things you needed. With that in mind, Pastor ended the service by saying, "Now let us give our prayer of thanks."

Cecil Buxton, who is more than somewhat hard of hearing, thought Pastor Woodstead said "prayer of tanks." He turned to his wife Leona and hollered, "WHAT?"

Harvey Delmar, sitting nearby, just smiled. Free advertising.

FALL

Of Mice and Martin

Last weekend was the annual Hay Festival in town, and it was quite a success, or what passes for a success in Frost Heaves. To begin with, the hay crop was awful this year, so we didn't get as much hay donated as we would have liked. Well, let's be honest, we only got one bale of hay. It was kind of a symbolic bale. (Walter Dunton, who thinks he is quite the wag, said we needed a "bale out." He should stick to making pizzas.)

But we went ahead anyway. We decided to liven things up this year by inviting the U.S. Marine Band to perform at the Hay Festival, which was very exciting. They didn't come, but we were excited just thinking about it.

Once again, we had the Miss Hay Bale contest. This year we had two contestants, Cindi Buxton and Jessica Willette. Since Jessica won last year, we didn't think we could give it to her again—not to mention that whole allergy thing—which only left Cindi, and we thought we should have at least one more person to make it a contest. Then, some smart-aleck nominated Viola Eldrich.

Viola is 82 and she has never been married, so she *is* a miss. Everyone thought that was pretty funny, but then

Viola decided to show them and she accepted the nomination. That was all well and good until it came to the swimsuit competition. The less said about that, the better. To make a long story even longer, Viola was chosen by popular vote to be Miss Hay Bale. This entitles her to go on to the county pageant next spring, but she's not sure she'll go. She's having her hip replaced and figures that might cramp her style. I guess we'll have to wait and see.

One new thing we did this year was a Hay Maze, like they do with them corn fields where they cut a maze in it and then let people loose to find their way out. That didn't work out so well. We had a lot of rain and not a lot of sunshine this year, so the hay was stunted and only came up to your knees, which made the maze pretty easy to figure out. We asked people not to look, but I think they did.

The turnout for the festival was good. A crowd of nearly two dozen people showed up, not including Edith Wyer's brother and sister-in-law, who had come to visit her and never really attended many of the events.

We don't actually get that many visitors in Frost Heaves, so when we do, we take notice. The other day, a well-dressed fellow walked into the diner and gazed around as if he was looking for someone. The owner, Bud, said, "Help you?"

"I'm supposed to meet a guy here and buy him breakfast," the fellow said. "But I don't know who he is."

Bud yelled out, "This fella is looking for a guy he don't know so he can buy him breakfast."

Well, every hand in the place went up. You got to be careful what you say when you are around Yankees.

Apart from the few human visitors, we do get a fair number of seasonal guests in Frost Heaves, mostly ants and mice; the ants arrive in the spring, and the mice come in the fall. Most folks get used to this, but some would rather not have the extra company.

Take Martin Kessler. He has been waging an ongoing battle against pests ever since he moved into the Carswell place. (The Kesslers have lived there for five years, but we still call it the Carswell place. In New England, a house isn't really yours until you move or pass on. This tends to confuse people from away, but we figure that in case of enemy attack, the invaders will be so confused that we'll have time to prepare our defenses. Of course, the only invaders we've ever seen around here are from New Jersey or Massachusetts, but we're not taking any chances.

Anyway, the old Carswell place was a favorite with the local pests. Last spring, when the first ants showed up, Martin set out some ant traps containing a substance called 2,2 dimethyl-1,3 benzodioxol-4-ol methylcarbamater (or "bendiocarb," as its friends call it). Apparently, bendiocarb is a big hit at ant buffets. The idea is, the ants carry the stuff back to their colonies, where it wipes them out. It's basically a weapon of ant mass-destruction.

At least, it's supposed to be. Either Martin's ants were on a bendiocarb-free diet, or else they could tell when something was too good to be true, because they just wrinkled their little ant noses at the traps and went out of their way to avoid them. Bear in mind, these are ants that, if they find a few grains of sugar, will have a big family reunion and invite all the second cousins they haven't seen in ages.

After a while, though, the ants went away. And before you knew it, fall arrived and so did the mice, moving in from their summer bungalows in the field next to the house. One morning, Martin found their little mouse calling cards under the sink, so he bought a mouse trap, put a dab of peanut butter on the business end of it, and figured he was all set.

The problem was, he forgot to check the trap before he left for work the next morning. He was in a big meeting about the eastern regional sales of flexible tubing when he got a call from his wife Sarah, who had come upon the trap, now occupied by an ex-mouse. Sarah is an animal lover, and she was somewhat less than pleased. Martin got an earful when he came home, along with explicit instructions to buy one of them new-fangled "doesn't kill 'em" traps.

Martin went to Dingle's Hardware, but Charlie Dingle only sells the old-fashioned traps, which don't leave any doubt as to the fate of the rodent in question. So Martin had to drive all the way to the Hardware Hutch in East Mildew, where they have two dozen different types of mouse traps, including the Mouse Mansion (a tin box with one-way doors that will hold up to 20 mice, if you believe the packaging), a trap that kills the mice with laser beams, and one that traps the mice and plays polka music until they kill themselves just to end the misery.

Being a sensitive, caring kind of guy—and because his wife had told him to—Martin went for a trap with a one-way door that let the mouse in for the bait, but wouldn't open until you flipped the trap over. This new trap worked pretty slick, too. For the first week or so, Martin caught a mouse every night. In the morning, he'd take the mouse out to the end of his driveway and dump it out.

Of course, the mice weren't stupid. They just kept coming back into the house. It was like an amusement park ride for them, with snacks included. They were practically lined up in the basement, waiting to have their turn.

This went on until Martin made the mistake of telling Millard Tuttle how many mice he'd caught. Millard didn't say much, but he mentioned that mice have been known to travel a couple of miles to get back to where they started. He told the story to the guys at the market, who have been laughing about "Martin's shuttle service" ever since.

That night, Martin woke to the sound of clunking noises coming from under the kitchen sink. You know that expression, quiet as a mouse? Whoever coined that never heard Martin's mice. A mariachi band should be so noisy.

When Martin checked the trap in the morning, it was empty. Then he noticed that the ant trap left over from spring had been pushed around and chewed on. Apparently, some mouse had been batting it around like a hockey puck, trying to get at the poison inside.

"OK," Martin said. "You want ant poison instead of cheese? Fine." He shook some of the bendiocarb into the mousetrap and reset it.

The next morning, he found a cute little, brown-eyed mouse in the trap. He pulled an empty cereal box from the trash to put the mouse in. At this point the mouse—who had previously wanted out of the trap—decided that given the options, maybe the trap wasn't that bad after all.

It developed Spider-Man-like ability to cling to the inside of the trap.

Martin eventually shook the mouse into the cereal box, which still had a few flakes at the bottom. "Eat up," he said. "We're going for a ride."

Given Millard's critique of his earlier mouse relocation efforts, Martin decided to deposit this one a little farther away than the end of his driveway. He decided to take it to Packer's Pond, which was on his way to work. He carried the cereal box out to his old Subaru, wedged it into the space between the front seats, and started it up.

Now, Martin's Subaru has lived through fifteen New England winters and two or three mufflerectomies, so it's more than a little noisy. Small children have been known to run indoors, covering their heads when he turns the key. So when the Subaru started rumbling, the mouse—which was already plenty agitated by the morning's activities—went into a panic. And when Martin put the car into gear, that mouse had had enough.

Maybe it was the adrenaline in his little mousie system. Maybe it was the bendiocarb. Whatever it was, as soon as the car started to move, that mouse shot out of the cereal box, clearing the top by about five inches, bounced off Martin's knee, and hit the floor running.

Let's just say Martin was not expecting this. As the mouse scurried around amongst the old coffee cups and McDonald's wrappers, Martin careened along, one eye on the road and one searching for the mouse. It's amazing how quickly a cute little mouse can become a mangy, disease-infested rodent when it's running around your car, ready to scoot up your pant leg. Martin sped to the pond as quickly as the Subaru would take him, then jumped out and threw open all the doors.

"All right! I know you're in there. Come on out."

Silence.

The Subaru had plenty of places for a mouse to hide, and Martin spent several minutes poking around, peeking beneath old hamburger wrappers and yelling "Aha!" But there was no sign of the mouse.

Finally, he opened the tailgate. The mouse—who had apparently been waiting for this moment—leaped to freedom, squeaking something that was probably the mouse equivalent of "Geronimo!"

Martin headed off to work, pondering the amazing effects of bendiocarb on a mouse's diet. Maybe he could begin marketing it as "Miracle Mouse—the Amazing Dietary Supplement for Mice." By the time he got to the office, he had an entire business plan drawn up.

He also decided he'd stop at Dingle's hardware store on the way home to buy a couple of old-fashioned mouse traps. He figured they were more natural, since they didn't use chemicals. And what Sarah didn't know wouldn't hurt her.

NEWS NUGGETS:
Daylight Saving

Once again, the town's selectmen have decided not to set our clocks back this fall along with the rest of the country. "We figure we're behind enough as it is," says Fred Kimball. "A few more years and maybe we'll catch up."

Also, starting this week at the library, Millard Tuttle will be displaying his rock collection. Millard has rocks from many famous places like Washington, D.C., Disneyland, Gettysburg, and more. Apart from that, they're just regular rocks, but it's still an impressive collection.

Up on the Roof

Now that it's autumn, folks are busy harvesting their gardens. As always, the gardens in town are overflowing with unwanted vegetables, probably a lot more this year because everyone was worried about the economy and planted extra in the spring.

Most of all, we have mountains of zucchini. I'm not sure why, but New Hampshire soil seems to be perfect for growing zucchini, a vegetable that even its own mother wishes would leave home. Around here, zucchini is practically an invasive species. The ladies in town have done just about everything you can think of to use up the zucchini—zucchini pickles, zucchini bread, zucchini relish, zucchini au gratin, au jus, and "Oh heck, we've still got more zucchini." To deal with the surplus, we set up a zucchini bank. We're stockpiling zucchini for distribution this winter to the less fortunate who might be in need.

By the by, for my money, the only vegetable more useless than zucchini is the eggplant. I figure God must have been joking when he thought that one up. The missus says, "Eggplant is delicious if you slice it, dip it in egg and bread crumbs, fry it, and top it with cheese and tomato sauce."

I says to her, "You could do that to a slice of life preserver and it would taste good. Got nothing to do with the eggplant."

Next weekend will be the monthly supper up to the Frost Heaves Community Church. It's a chicken dinner this time, with zucchini casserole and apple crisp for dessert. I should warn you that the apple crisp is not really all that crisp. The ladies have been using Alvira Thompkin's recipe for years, and since her daughters Mavis and Avis are in charge of the church suppers, the ladies will keep using that recipe until the sisters pass away or Jesus returns, whichever comes first. If we insisted on truth in advertising, they'd have to call it Apple Limp, which doesn't sound that appetizing, does it?

Entertainment at the supper will be provided by The Travelling Mercies, a singing group made up of Bob and Betty Mercy and their children Brenda, Brian, Billy, Belinda, and Roy. One of those children was not exactly planned, if you catch my drift.

Speaking of children, the kids are back at school up at the Frost Heaves Academy. There was quite a bit of excitement on the first day of school. When the janitor arrived to open up in the morning, he found a pig running down the halls with a number 1 painted on its side. A little while later, some girls found another pig in their locker room with a number 4 painted on it. The lunch ladies cornered pig number 2 in the cafeteria—that one was kind of panicky, maybe because it knew the ladies were making ham sandwiches for lunch. Before they corralled it, that pig left an unfavorable review of the lunch menu in the middle of the cafeteria floor.

Needless to say, the kids were all excited by this activity. It was a whole lot more interesting than anything the teachers had planned for that day.

A little while later, Chester Franklin called the police station to say that some of his pigs were missing. Chief Spaulding told Chester he was already on it, though he didn't say they were still looking for pig #3. Chester tends to be protective of his pigs and the chief didn't want him to worry.

As an aside, I should say that this prank was more creative than anything we did back in the day when I was at the academy. I enjoyed my time in school, but my teachers always said that I wasn't living up to my potential. I tried to explain to them that my potential was a whole lot less than they imagined, and time seems to have borne me out on that score.

The other interesting thing that happened recently was a meeting in Center Frost Heaves. I don't know as I have explained that the north part of Frost Heaves is what we call Center Frost Heaves, or sometimes Upper Frost Heaves. It's separated a bit from the rest of town, and it's actually the oldest part of town. It's also the place with the nicest houses, where the few fairly well-to-do residents live. These folks generally like to distance themselves from the rest of Frost Heaves. In fact, they act like they aren't actually part of Frost Heaves.

For quite some time, folks in that part of town have thought about seceding from Frost Heaves and forming their own town. The biggest problem is that they can't decide what to call it. Someone suggested Centertown, but that just seemed kind of generic. Someone else said they should name it after one of the Presidents, but most of the good ones are already taken—Washington, Jefferson, Lincoln—and no one got too excited about the idea of a Fillmore or a Pierce, New Hampshire, especially given our native son Franklin's less-than-stellar performance in the White House. Folks from other parts of town suggested the secessionists call themselves Snootyville, or some other names I can't repeat here. Anyway, no one could agree on what to call this new town, so the meeting broke up, and I guess they're going to be stuck with us for a while.

A few years back, one person did actually manage to secede from the town of Frost Heaves. Dexter Acworth decided he was sick of his property taxes going up every year. He lives on Crabby Creek Road, in a house he inherited from his grandfather Dexter, Sr., who may have been responsible for the name Crabby Creek. He made Ebeneezer Scrooge look like a model of friendliness and generosity.

Anyway, Dexter's place is right on the border between Frost Heaves and East Mildew, the next town over. The taxes are lower in East Mildew, so Dexter went to the town fathers there and said he wanted to be in their town. They were all for it. Of course, folks in Frost Heaves were kind of peeved, but it turns out there was nothing they could do to stop him.

So now the town line on the east side of Frost Heaves runs in a straight line except where it jogs around Dexter's house. The folks across the street and on either side of him live in Frost Heaves, but Dexter lives in East Mildew. He gets his mail from the East Mildew post office, and he goes to the East Mildew town meeting.

Of course, come the first big snowfall last winter, Dexter was a little surprised to look out and see that the road had been plowed everywhere except right in front of his house—the guys just lifted the plow as they went by. The town fathers have told him they're willing to accept him back into Frost Heaves whenever he comes to his senses, but if you know Dexter, that isn't going to happen any time soon.

Dexter has certainly had his share of troubles lately. We had a big wind a while back that blew some shingles off his barn roof, so Dexter decided to get up there and fix 'em. It's a steep roof and Dexter isn't getting any younger, which made him a little nervous about undertaking the project, so he decided he'd better hitch up a safety rope. He tied it around his waist, then he tied the other end to the back end of his car, climbed up the ladder and went over to the far side of the roof. (Got the picture? This is important: Dexter on one side, car on the other side, rope running over the peak.)

Dexter was working away up there for an hour or so when he heard the front door open and his wife Annie come out of the house. He didn't think anything of that, till he heard the car being started.

It seems Dexter hadn't told her what he was up to, and she hadn't noticed the rope tied to the back of the car. Dexter yelled, but she was in the car, so she didn't hear him. The next thing you know, Dexter was being dragged up the roof towards the ridge, hollering bloody blue murder.

At that point, Annie thought maybe she had heard something, so she stopped and rolled down the window. But Dexter had stopped yelling and was doing his best

Houdini imitation, trying to get the rope untied from around himself. Fortunately, he managed to undo the knot just as Annie started the car up again. Unfortunately, the rope got tangled around the ladder and pulled it over before it untangled. Annie headed to town, trailing the rope behind her and unaware of the pickle she'd left Dexter in.

There he was, perched up on the roof, with no way to get down. That's when he remembered that Annie was going to her sister's over to East Mildew for the day and wouldn't be back till late that night.

Dexter does not have a cell phone, and even if he did, it wouldn't have done him much good. As I explained earlier, the chances of getting decent cell phone reception in Frost Heaves are about as good as the chances of seeing a pyramid, maybe less. Besides, there was no one to call. From his perch up on the roof, Dexter could see pretty much the whole town. He could see the cruiser up at the Frost Heaves Academy, where Chief Spaulding was looking for that last pig. He could see someone on Main Street dropping a basket of green vegetables off on someone's porch. He could see the guys from the volunteer fire department converging at the station and he wondered what that was about.

What it was about was a mutual aid call that had come in over the computer, asking them to go to East Angus to help with a fire. They plugged the street address into the GPS and headed out with the truck, but right away they were confused. The computer told them to head west towards Vermont, but East Angus is *east* of Frost Heaves. Still, they figured the GPS knew what it was doing, until fifteen minutes later when it told them to head north. Now they were really confused.

Finally, they called mutual aid. It took a while to get things straightened out. It turned out that the call was for East Angus, *Quebec*, not East Angus, New Hampshire. The East Angus in Canada is a four-hour drive from Frost Heaves. Apparently, the computer looked for towns near East Angus and stumbled upon Frost Heaves. Maybe you've heard the expression, "To err is human, but if you really want to screw up, you need a computer."

A couple of the volunteers still wanted to go on the call, but their wives would have killed them if they were gone that long. So they headed back home, and as they came into town they went down Crabby Creek Road, where they heard someone yelling. They pulled over and saw Dexter sitting up on the roof of his house.

Mickey Edwards, our fire chief, yelled up to him. "Dexter, what are you doing up there?"

"Watching the sunset, what do you think I'm doing?" Dexter yelled back. "Bring that ladder over here and help me down." This was probably not the tone for Dexter to take with the one guy in town who could help him just then.

Mickey thought a moment. "Well, I'd like to, Dexter, but we can't cross town lines unless we get a mutual aid call. So you'll have to call the fire department in your town first."

Needless to say, Dexter wasn't in any position to call anyone, other than the few names he called Mickey and the other guys as they drove the firetruck away. He sat up there for another hour or so. Later on, Mickey did come back, in his own car, and put Dexter's ladder back up so

Dexter could climb down. Dexter thanked him, but I don't think his heart was really in it.

Meanwhile, up at the school, Chief Spaulding had spent all day looking for that fourth pig, the one labeled #3. There was no sign of it, and at the end of the day, he decided he better bite the bullet and call Chester Franklin to give him the bad news.

"Chester," he said, "I got to tell you, we were only able to find three of your pigs."

"Well," Chester said, "I'm only missing three pigs."

It turns out there never was a pig #3. That was part of the kids' plan all along. As I say, those youngsters are a whole lot more creative than I ever was. It gives me great hope for their future. I just hope they live up to their potential.

NEWS NUGGETS:
Fall Specials

For a limited time, Chef Walter at the Frost Heaves House of Pizza is offering a Fall Foliage pizza. It comes with green peppers, but while you're eating it, he comes to the table and sprinkles red and yellow peppers on it. It's a little messy, but it does taste good.

Meanwhile, at the Peabody Tavern, Elwood Peabody has come up with a special seasonal drink that combines pumpkin liqueur and applejack. He calls it a Jack-o-Lantern because when you drink it, you feel lit up inside and your eyes start to glow.

Not Quite Cricket

When Millard Tuttle was a boy, he loved crickets. Every year, as soon as it was warm enough to leave his bedroom window open, Millard would lie in bed and listen to summer's opening musical act coming from the field beside the farmhouse: cricket calls echoing over the new grass and young frogs peeping from the banks of the creek that meandered past the field.

But Millard's attitude changed back when he bought the old Pitman place on Lazybrook Road. For some reason, that house is a cricket magnet. Every year around the second week in August, the crickets migrate from the fields, drawn to the old clapboard manse as if they were returning to their ancestral homestead, heeding the call of an ancient memory laid down by their forebears in the dim reaches of the past. Or maybe they just want to get warm.

At any rate, the crickets find their way into the house through chinks in the clapboards and cracks at the top of the foundation. Millard has even caught them hopping up the steps, as if they hoped to be invited through the front door. At least the peepers had the decency to stay outside.

The first August in their new home, the crickets took Millard and Millie by surprise. No one warned them—by the time Pearl Pitman went off to the nursing home, she couldn't remember her own kids' names, let alone remembering to warn the new people about the crickets.

At first, Millard and Millie took the crickets in stride. Cricket season only lasted a few weeks, and after all, a cricket on the hearth was supposed to be good luck. But Millard soon found that anything more than one cricket was a nuisance. Three crickets justified an insanity plea in a murder case.

After twenty years in the Pitman place, Millard's annual battle with the crickets had become a ritual. On those August nights, Millard would lie in bed waiting for the tournament to begin. The crickets waited too, till the house was quiet and all the lights were out. Millie just covered her head with a pillow. She had given up.

One night, as on every other night, it was a single cricket that began the contest.

"Reek...reek...reek."

The crickets always appeared one at a time, which made Millard wonder how they decided whose turn it was. "You got the short straw, Felix. It's your turn."

For those of you who slept through eighth-grade science class, here's a reminder: crickets make noise by rubbing their front wings together. The result is a high-pitched sound that, as part of an outdoor chorus, is the essence of a New England summer. Inside a house, the noise is an all-natural alarm clock, every bit as annoying as those darned electronic ones.

"Reek...reek...reek."

Millard sat up on the edge of the bed. As always, the chirping stopped.

Millard held his breath. He was used to the routine by now. The crickets sensed when he was coming and knew enough to shut up for a while. Eventually, though…

"Reek…reek…reek."

Millard tiptoed, still in his nightshirt, to the kitchen. He grabbed the flashlight from its place on the kitchen counter and picked up the nearest piece of footwear, a Timberland boot creased with age, the toe blown out.

From the kitchen drawer, Millard pulled out two spoons and lay down on the kitchen floor. Long experience had taught him where the crickets hid—in the crack between the baseboard and the floor—and he had developed a foolproof method for sending them on to their eternal reward.

Millard shone the flashlight along the crack until he spotted the culprit. It should be said that this was not Jiminy Cricket. This was a New England cockroach, a malign creature with twitching antennae that lurked in the darkness, waiting to inflict psychological torture on the residents of 27 Lazybrook Road.

In the past, Millard had tried holding the flashlight in his mouth so he could keep the cricket in its beam like a criminal skittering against the brick wall of a penitentiary, but his chin kept bumping the floor. These days, he rested the flashlight on the floor where it cast a general glow over the scene.

By now, the cricket had stopped chirping. Millard stuck the handle of a spoon in the baseboard crack several inches ahead of the cricket. The second spoon went into the crack on its other side. Millard slid the spoons together, the cricket scurrying along the crack till it found itself bracketed, unable to go anywhere except to leave the security of the crack.

Millard gave the spoons a final push and the cricket skittered out onto the linoleum. Millard grabbed the boot and brought it down on the cricket with a "Hah!" and a satisfying crunch. He had tried other cricket smashing tools—books, crumbled paper towels—but the boot had just the right feel, good leverage, and he didn't mind getting cricket guts on it. As violent as this seems, it was actually a concession. Millard had become so expert with the spoons that he could have killed the cricket right in the crack, crunching it between the spoon handles. (Once—his moment of glory—he'd actually killed a cricket with *one* spoon.) But it seemed more sportsmanlike to draw them out into the open and kill them with the boot—the cricket equivalent of hunting with a bow and arrow rather than a scoped rifle. At least that gave the cricket a fighting chance—albeit a slim one—to skitter around the spoons and back into the safety of the crack.

Millard went back to bed, pulled the chain on the bedside lamp, and snuggled up against Millie's back. The air was cool, but it was warm under the quilt, perfect sleeping weather.

"Reek…"

Millard's eyes snapped open. He had been killing crickets long enough to judge their size by the tone of the chirp, and this was a small one.

He sat on the edge of the bed, listening. As always, the cricket fell silent.

He waited. This was a cagey one. It knew Millard was waiting for him. But Millard could wait, too. He was patient. Oh yes, he was patient.

The clock in the hallway ticked for a full minute.

"Reek…"

The sound had come from the hallway. Millard rose and grabbed a slipper. Occasionally, a cricket would hide under the hall rug. Millard had learned to sneak up, hoist the rug, and smash the bug before it could escape. But the hallway was cricket-free. He waited. Another minute passed.

"Reek …"

The cellar. He opened the door and stared into the darkness. Millard's was a typical New England cellar, a place you hardly wanted to go in the daytime, let alone the middle of the night.

Silence.

He turned on the cellar light and crept down the stairs. There were a million places a cricket could hide down there. He shone the flashlight in the corners and investigated the stairs leading up to the bulkhead. But there was no cricket.

"Reek…"

The sound had come from upstairs. The little bugger had tricked him, sneaking into the house from the cellar landing while Millard prowled around below.

He stormed up the stairs and closed the door. "All right. Now you're in my territory, buster."

Silence.

Millard paced the hallway to the front room, shining the flashlight in crevices, behind furniture, under chairs. "Come on, you chicken. Show yourself."

Silence.

He went to the kitchen table and sat, breathing hard. He would catch this one if it took him all night.

"Reek…"

The hallway again. Somehow, he had missed it.

He wasn't taking any chances this time. He crept to the hall in slow motion, his feet touching the floorboards with no more noise than a mouse would make, stepping over any boards that he knew would creak.

The process took him several minutes. Finally, he stood before the cellar door.

"Reek…"

He'd been wrong. It was still in the cellar, behind the door.

He peeled the door open so slowly, so silently that it would have taken time-lapse photography to capture the motion.

Silence.

He shone the light at the top of the stairs.

"Reek…"

The sound had come from overhead. He flashed the flashlight at the ceiling. If the cricket was up there, he would have to tear the ceiling down to get at it. But he would do it. By God, he would do it if he had to.

A red light from the smoke alarm glowed in the darkness. Millard waited.

"Reek…"

It was inside the smoke alarm. He grabbed the cover, ready to snap it off and stomp the cricket when it fell out.

He snapped, twisted, and pulled the cover off. The only thing that fell out was a 2-year-old battery, hanging limply from its connecting wires.

"Reek," the battery whimpered, signaling the end of its useful life.

Millard yanked the battery out, tossed it in the trash, and stumbled back to bed.

Millie rolled over, mumbling, "Did you get it?"

"Ayuh."

Millie was asleep in a minute. Millard lay staring at the ceiling, considering whether he would tell her the truth in the morning. Maybe not. A man didn't need to give his wife any more ammunition to prove he was an idiot. In the morning, he would go to Dingles and buy a new battery. For now, he lay in the darkness, basking in the calm stillness of the old house, the gentle breathing of his wife beside him, the blessed, blessed silence.

"Reek…reek…reek…"

NEWS NUGGETS:
Turkey Tours

At the recent meeting of the FRED council, Walter Dunton presented a new idea for promoting the town of Frost Heaves. "Down at Cape Cod, they do whale watches and dolphin tours, which gave me an idea," says Walter, who proposed that the town offer wild turkey tours. "We'd get a few old golf carts and take people around on the back roads," he explained. "We could even set up a turkey cam so folks could watch from home." Walter did a mockup of an ad for the turkey tours, which had the tagline, "In Frost Heaves, you're guaranteed to see turkeys." To which the other committee members responded, "That's for sure."

Welcome, Presidential Doubtfuls

Every election year, we get a bumper crop of politicians traipsing through New Hampshire. At first, most of them claim they are not running for president, as if they had a sudden urge to travel halfway across the country in search of maple syrup or a good ham and bean supper.

They aren't fooling us. These are folks hoping to use their successful stint as head of the Bowling Alley Safety Commission as a springboard to the Oval Office. Most of them have about as much chance of being president as my cat Lena, maybe less.

Anyway, in Frost Heaves, we decided to take advantage of this situation and offer a special travel package to all these White House wannabees. We call it the "Not Officially a Presidential Entrant" package, or NOPE for short.

The package will begin with an official welcome from our state senator, Lester Milfoil. Lester has a 20-year history of not taking strong positions on anything. Consequently, you can list his legislative achievements on a gum wrapper—one of the little sugarless ones, not the full-sized pieces—and you'll still have room for a couple of phone numbers. Lester is most proud of his work on choosing the state muffin—blueberry—though he managed to be absent for the controversial vote on the state amphibian (the Red-spotted newt).

We had originally planned for Lester to give each candidate the key to the city, but we can't find it. Edith Wyer says Alfred Cooper had it last, but Alfred says no. "Besides," Edith says, "I don't think we should be handing out keys to a bunch of strangers anyway."

We'll start the tour with breakfast at the Bluebell Diner, where the candidates will rub elbows with Mr. and Mrs. John Doe—unless it's a Thursday. On Thursdays, John plays checkers at the senior center in East Mildew and Jane has Bible study at the First Church of the Last Hope in Milliwillitockset. The other point of the breakfast is to make sure the candidates have the intestinal fortitude to be president. Remember back when George H.W. Bush tossed his cookies all over the Japanese prime minister's shoes? We don't want a repeat of that. We figure if politicians can handle the food at the Bluebell Diner, they're ready for anything.

Then we'll give the candidates a tour of local industry. Frost Heaves doesn't actually have much in the way of industry—personal or otherwise—but politicians always want photo ops. We'll take them to the Frost Heaves House of Pizza, where Chef Walter is serving his newest creation, brown bread pizza with weenie franks and cheddar cheese. Then it's off to Charlie Dingle's hardware store ("Serving mostly satisfied customers off and on since 1957"), the Bait and Beauty Salon (featuring a Manicure and Minnows package), and Herb Cullen's farm stand, offering a Buy-One, Get-One zucchini special.

We'll end up at Homer Andrews' farm. Homer has a Holstein named Henrietta that was born with the profile of the Old Man of the Mountain on her side, and politicians just love to have their picture taken with her. What they don't know is that the Old Man shape has changed as Henrietta has grown. These days, it looks more like a map of Mississippi, so Homer has taken to touching it up with shoe polish. That doesn't bother us—all the politicians wear makeup these days, so why shouldn't Henrietta?

The day will end with a Town Hall meeting and a free bean supper, paid for by the candidate. We figure this will ensure that folks will show up to meet the candidate instead of staying home to watch Dancing with the Desperate Bachelor Chefs on TV.

We'll charge the politicians for the NOPE package the way the government does. We'll give them a price and take their credit cards, but when they get their statement, the price might be two, three, or even four times what we said. We're hoping they'll take the hint. Call us dreamers.

As for me, I am sticking by my longstanding decision not to run for elected office. I figure the best way for me to do my patriotic duty and serve my country is just to stay out of it. However, I do have some ideas for solving our state's problems, which I am happy to share.

You know how the government pays farmers subsidies not to plant things? I think we should do the same thing with politicians. We should pay them not to run for office. I know, it sounds like a waste, but I think we'll save money in the long run. You know, the more people you have in an organization, the greater the chance that one of them will come up with a really stupid idea.

Here in New Hampshire, we have 400 state representatives, so you do the math.

To limit the damage, I think we should put our representatives on retainer and send them home. Then we can call them back if we need them to vote on anything important, like Psoriasis Awareness Month or making zucchini bread the state pastry. Again, this will probably be a lot cheaper than having them sit around all the time with nothing to do. Ask any parent of teenagers. Personally, I like the idea of getting paid not to do something. I'd try it myself, but I'm already not doing anything.

Speaking of stupid ideas, some of our state senators seem to think increased gambling is the way to solve our financial problems. Frankly, if you think gambling is a way to make money, you haven't got the brains God gave rhubarb. If they insist on gambling, let's do it the way we do in Frost Heaves: bingo. But here's the twist. We will make everyone play. That's right, Universal Mandatory Bingo. The prizes would be stuff people have tucked away in their attics and cellars, like that old bureau you got from your Aunt Ida that you hate but can't toss out because it's a family heirloom. This would save money on prizes, and it would also cut down on the number of yard sales in our state, which has reached epidemic proportions lately.

A lot of folks are worried about illegal immigration. I'm not—my ancestors came here in the 1600s without an invitation, so I think we ought to keep the welcome mat out as much as possible. However, I am worried about our northern border. New Hampshire has a vast, extended 58-mile border with our northern neighbor, Canada, and exactly one border crossing checkpoint. So far, we've been getting along OK with Canada—except for the War of 1812 business—but that unprotected border worries me. What's to stop a Canadian moose from stepping over the line and taking work away from our native-born moose? And what about a moose cow that wanders over the border and has a calf here? Does that make it an American moose? I don't have a solution, I just bring up the question.

Finally, I think there's entirely too much cussing going on these days. If folks want to swear, that's OK, but I think they should pay for the privilege with an annual swearing license. There would be varying levels; folks who only wanted to say the not-so-bad words would get a beginner's permit for a reasonable price. The real potty-mouths would need an expert license, and it would cost quite a bit more. There are a couple of guys in Frost Heaves who could pay for a new addition to the elementary school all by themselves.

Well, those are my ideas. Feel free to pass them on to any politicians you may see passing through.

Police Log: Bird Alert

On Thursday, police responded to a 911 call at the home of Velma Thurston. Velma denied placing the call, though she lives alone. Officer Lamott overheard Velma's mynah bird Thurston calling, "Help! 911! Help!" Under questioning, Velma admitted that she had taught Thurston to peck out 911 in case of emergency because she didn't want to pay for a medical alert system. According to Velma, "I guess he thinks not getting his afternoon treat is an emergency, the little bugger."

Close Encounters

As with most great ideas, there is some disagreement about who thought up the Frost Heaves foliage contest. Walter Dunton claims it was his idea, but Edith Wyer says he wasn't even in the room at the time. This was during a meeting of the Frost Heaves Regional Economic Development council, where we were still trying to think of ways to promote the town.

Walter Dunton said we should do something to take advantage of all the tourists who come to New England in the fall, which wasn't the worst idea to come out of the FRED council. Autumn in New England is a wonderful time of year, one that makes even a town like Frost Heaves look good. There's a crispness in the air, like a Macintosh apple just picked from a tree at the orchard on Swede's Hill. At the farmstand, Herb Cullen always has pumpkins of all shapes and sizes, along with mums, cornstalks, and ornamental gourds. The days are still warm but the nights start to get chilly. The woolly-bear caterpillars come out with their predictions of how hard a winter it's going to be.

(As a side note, folks have lots of ways of predicting what kind of winter we're going to have. They'll look at the acorn crop, or how bushy the squirrels' tails are, or the stripes on the wooly-bear caterpillars. But in Frost Heaves, we have a foolproof method of telling what kind of winter we're in for: Albert Trombley's eyebrows. Albert has these massive eyebrows that make woolly bears look anorexic. Each of his eyebrows should have its own zip code. A while ago, someone figured out that you could predict the coming winter by the size of Albert's eyebrows; the bushier his eyebrows, the longer winter was going to be. This may sound like nonsense to you, but that's just because you don't put any faith in the scientific method.)

(And a side, side note. Even professional weather predictors aren't that good at it. When they tell you all heck's going to break loose, you can relax. When they say it's going to be partly cloudy, you better get ready; the next thing you know, you'll have twelve inches of "partly cloudy" in your driveway. And will you get any kind of explanation or apology from the weather people? No, you will not. They just go on as if nothing happened. I guess being a weather person means never having to say you're sorry.)

Anyway, everyone agreed that some kind of fall promotion would be good, but what? Then someone—and again, Edith says it wasn't Walter—suggested they hold a Most Beautiful Tree contest to pick the tree with the best foliage in town. There wouldn't be any prize, just bragging rights, which we put a lot of store by in Frost Heaves. (We don't have much to brag about, which is why we make a big deal of it on the rare occasions when we can.) Everyone on the committee agreed this was a good idea, and best of all, it wouldn't cost anything.

"How are we going to let people know about it?" Edith asked.

The members kicked that question around for a while until Dave Miller suggested we have a hotline that tourists could call for information about the town and events like the foliage contest. Herb Cullen suggested that whoever answered the phone should say, "Tenk you veddy much for calling de Frost Heaves help lion," with an Indian accent so people would think it was a bigger operation than it actually was. Edith squashed that idea with a withering glare, but the basic idea of the help line was approved.

Unfortunately for Edith, she was assigned to staff the help line, since she was always on duty in the town hall anyway, which meant we wouldn't have to hire anyone else to answer the phone. Dave Miller set up a new number for the help line that was patched through to Edith's phone. She didn't really want the job—she already had plenty to do as town clerk—but it wasn't that much work. It turns out that not that many people want to visit Frost Heaves, foliage notwithstanding. The only folks who did call were people from town who couldn't find their meatloaf recipe or wanted a ride to the fish market in Milliwillitockset.

Then one Friday, the phone rang and Edith saw the help line light up. "Frost Heaves help line, Edith speaking."

A man's voice barked, "Yeah, this is Frank D'Antonio from Hampstead, Long Island."

"Yes?" Edith said, not sure why she needed the caller's full name and place of residence.

"We're thinking about coming up there to catch the foliage, so I wanna know when the leaves are gonna change color."

Edith had worked up a sheet with answers to the questions she was going to be asked most often, and that one was top of the list. "Well, sir," she said, reading from the sheet, "the turning of the leaves varies, depending on the weather conditions, such as how much precipitation we've had—"

"Yeah, yeah, yeah. But when does it happen?"

Edith took a deep breath. She did not take kindly to being interrupted, but she was mindful of her position as the face of Frost Heaves tourism, or at least the voice of it. "Generally speaking, the leaves turn during the first or second week of October," she said, her tone even.

"OK, but what about this year?"

"This year, we're estimating that peak foliage will occur in the second week of October."

"Great. What day?"

She wasn't sure she'd heard him right. "What day?"

"Yeah, cause we gotta make a reservation, you know. We don't want to show up and find out we missed it."

"I'm afraid there are millions of trees, so it's impossible to tell—"

"Yeah, yeah. I know, it's probably some big local secret. But you can tell me. I won't tell no one else, honest."

Edith glared at the phone over the tops of her pearl-rimmed glasses, which anyone from town could have told the caller was not a good sign. Somehow, though, she managed to keep her annoyance in check. "Sir, there's no way to know—"

"Come on, lady, gimme a break. You want people to come up there or not? I'm not gonna go all the way to

New Hampshire if I'm not gonna get to see the leaves actually changing color, so what day do they turn?"

Edith took a deep breath. "Tuesday."

"All right. That wasn't so hard, was it? Now, what time of day?"

"Excuse me?"

"What time of day do the leaves turn? Morning, afternoon?"

Struggling now to control herself, Edith resorted to the answer sheet again. "The process of changing colors happens over a period—"

"Yeah, yeah, yeah. Look, Barb and I went all the way up to Canada to see the tide coming into the Bay of Fundy, and we got there at the wrong time. How was I supposed to know it only happens every six hours? 'You could 'a called,' Barb says. So here I am. I'm calling, I'm asking. When do the leaves turn?"

Edith's lips tightened into a thin line. "2 p.m."

"Great. Now we're getting somewhere. So that's Tuesday, at 2 p.m. Next question: Where do you keep the moose?"

Edith's irritation was momentarily checked by her confusion. "Moose?"

"Yeah. We keep hearing about all the moose up there and we wanna see one. So where do we go?"

She was sorely tempted to tell this gentleman where he could go, but held her tongue. "One moment, please."

She punched the hold button, walked to the coffee maker, and poured her second cup of the day. Edith drinks her coffee black, despite it being only slightly less caustic than battery acid. She took a heartening sip, pondering the worst possible route to send someone on a wild goose chase—or wild moose chase, as the case may be. She took her time getting back to her desk and punched the hold button.

"Moose Hotline. How may I help you?"

The Most Beautiful Tree contest turned out to be one of the most popular events sponsored by the FRED council, better even than the Road Kill Meat Raffle and the Adopt a Heave program. Dozens of people registered their trees, and the council drew up a map for folks to follow so they could vote on their favorites.

Earl Hadley, who lives on Hadley Hill Road, figured he was a shoo-in to win the contest. Earl has one of the oldest trees in town in front of his house, a glorious old sugar maple that it would take three people to wrap their arms around. That tree is in the neighborhood of 150 to 200 years old and was just a teenager when the boys from Frost Heaves marched off to Gettysburg. The tree reached its prime about the time the Titanic sank and hit middle age just as Neil Armstrong took that small step off the lunar lander.

These days, Earl's tree is a stately senior citizen, its branches gnarled and arthritic, one or two of them dropping off every year. People have told Earl he should have the tree trimmed, but that costs money and Earl is tighter than a 32-inch belt on a 36-inch waist. "Mother Nature will take care of it," he always says.

Despite Earl's neglect, the tree puts on a wonderful show every fall, its leaves turning from green to plum red, then to orange and burnt gold before falling in showers onto Earl's yard. The problem is, the leaves don't stay in Earl's yard. His house sits on a knoll with a westerly breeze that sweeps over it most of the year. In the fall, the wind scatters Earl's leaves down into the yard of his neighbor, Homer Cratchet, where they pile up against the house, as high as the sills of the dining room windows. Homer has tried suggesting to Earl that he should rake the leaves or even, God forbid, pay some youngster to do the job. But Earl just shrugs. "Mother Nature put 'em there, Mother Nature will take care of it," he says. And Mother Nature—or that westerly wind—always does.

At any rate, Earl's tree was the leading contender to win the Most Beautiful Tree contest. When folks called the Frost Heaves help line, Edith Wyer always told them to be sure and check it out, as it was a stunner.

Frank and Barb D'Antonio arrived in Frost Heaves on a Tuesday that was, just as Edith had predicted, the peak of foliage season. The drive had taken them six hours, what with stopping for lunch and rest stops every hour because—according to Frank—Barb's bladder is the size of a kid's juice box.

They had made reservations at the Peabody Inn, the least expensive place they could find, and when they checked in, they knew why. According to the numbers nailed beside the front door, the Inn had been built in 1783—neither of them could understand why anyone would advertise how old their place was, as if that was something to be proud of—and it looked as if nothing had been done to the place since 1783. The Inn's owner registered them, and he seemed especially proud of the historic hand-painted murals on the walls, which looked to Frank like Egypt after most of the major plagues had passed through.

Frank and Barb slept soundly, despite a mattress that seemed to have been stuffed with dried cabbage leaves. In the morning, they enjoyed—well, tolerated—a 3-star breakfast in the Inn's lounge., Then they headed off with the map the lady on the help line had sent them, a meandering route that took them past what it called the highlights of Frost Heaves, including a scenic road that seemed to go nowhere, a tree with a cannonball stuck in it, and a plaque marking the first person from New Hampshire to be captured during the Civil War.

"What's next?" Frank asked Barb, who was studying the map.

"Turn left on Scoopnagle Road."

"We were just on Scoopnagle Road."

"No, that was *Old* Scoopnagle Road. This is different."

"What, they run outta names up here and hadda start reusing names or something?"

"I dunno, maybe."

The next item of interest was a farm with a cow that supposedly had markings resembling the Old Man of the Mountain.

They rounded a bend and the farm came into view. It sat at the base of Mount Monadnock, surrounded by open pastures. Up ahead, a farmer whose wrinkled face appeared to have been made from a dried apple stood by an open gate, watching as his cows—several dozen of them—meandered through the gate, across the road, and into the field on the other side, a process that was proceeding at the rate of cold molasses pouring from a jug, maybe slower.

Frank pulled up to the parade and stopped. "Come on, come on," he muttered, giving his horn a little beep to speed up the action. One or two cows turned to gaze placidly in Frank's direction, but the farmer did not. (Homer Andrews, the farmer in question, only has two operating speeds: slow and—if anyone tries to rush him—slower.)

What felt like an hour later, the cows completed their exodus to the other field, several of them having stopped to tell Frank what they thought of his attitude by leaving a deposit in the middle of the road.

"Finally," Frank said, plowing through the poop.

"Ewww!" Barb said. "Why did you drive through it?"

"What was I supposed to do, back up and go all the way around or something?"

"I don't know—"

"Or maybe I was supposed to get out and shovel it out of the way, first. Oh, wait, I forgot to bring a shovel."

"Never mind."

Not wanting to talk about it anymore, Barb pulled a CD from her purse and stuck it into the car's stereo. A wailing sound emerged from the speakers, as if someone was tormenting a cat with a cello.

"What the hell is that?" Frank said.

"That's Lisa's CD." Lisa was Barb's niece, who had dropped out of law school to pursue her passion for music, which she called "avant-avant-garde." Most of Lisa's fans—and this was a select group—downloaded her music from the Internet, but she had produced a few physical CDs as a concession to fogies like her aunt who were stuck with old technology.

"You call that music?" Frank said, grimacing.

Barb shrugged. She didn't particularly care for Lisa's music either. Celine Dion, she wasn't. "Well, at least she didn't use her real name."

"Whadya mean?"

"She has a stage name. Ushi."

"Sushi?" Frank barked. "What the hell—"

"Not sushi, _Ushi_. It's Japanese, I think."

Frank shook his head. "That makes about as much sense as the music."

She ignored him and read the CD cover. "Ushi—Songs of Delight and Despair."

"Don't tell me," he snickered. "This is despair."

"Be nice," said Fran, who had always supported her niece's somewhat erratic life choices. "It's not so bad. It's…soothing."

"Right. A hot tub and a glass of Merlot, that's soothing. Sinatra on the stereo, that's soothing. This is painful."

As if to emphasize the point, he rolled down all four windows, hoping the wind would drown out the low moans emanating from the speakers.

Barb responded by cranking up the music. And on they drove.

A quarter mile away, a full-grown male moose—known to his buddies as Grunt and weighing in at three-quarters of a ton—stood gazing at the road, his head sweeping lazily back and forth. Grunt was a respected senior citizen in the moose community, having survived twenty New Hampshire winters and just as many hunting seasons. He had spent most of the summer alone in the deep woods, grazing on twigs and willow bark, bathing in secluded lakes, and generally taking it easy. Toward the end of the summer, he and the other bulls had gathered for their annual get-together before rutting season, a ritual that consisted of circling each other, staging mock battles ("You want a piece of me? Huh? Do ya?") and tearing up trees and shrubs to demonstrate how tough they were.

When the weather turned cool, Grunt had headed down to the lower woods by the rivers and streams where the girls generally hung out, hoping to get lucky. So far, he'd struck out, despite leaving his pee calling card over a wide range, digging a scrape to bathe in his own unique cologne, and beating the bushes—literally—to announce his arrival and warn any other bulls to back off.

Just now, he'd come upon one of those long, thin stretches of rock-hard ground, the grey-black kind that cut through the woods like a knife and smelled of tar. These stretches were generally empty, but sometimes large buzzing insects flew along them, sunlight shining off their carapaces in the daytime, their bug eyes beaming out ahead of them at night. Every now and then, one of these creatures would run into a moose, and the bug usually came out the loser in the encounter. Nevertheless, Grunt always took his time before crossing such a strip; he was really looking forward to mating this year and didn't want to get sidelined by any knee injuries before the big event.

From off in the distance came a low moan and Grunt turned to gaze toward it. There, coming towards him, was one of the bugs, its humming vibrating through the hard ground. But there was another sound as well, one that made his juices flow and his moosehood quiver. He raised his head and cocked his ears. Yes, that was it, the sweet, siren song of a moose cow in heat. At least, he thought it was. At his age, his hearing wasn't all it used to be.

Down the road, Frank had had enough. He was about to turn off the CD, but stopped when he saw the moose standing in the road—a big one, with antlers wider than the car.

"Look," Barb shouted. "A moose!"

"I see it, I see it." He slowed down, assuming that the moose would get out of the way as they came closer. But it didn't. It just stood there, staring at them.

Frank slowed down more. He was crawling now, but fortunately there was no one else around, just them and the moose on the open highway.

He stopped a dozen yards away from the moose and turned the CD off. At this distance, he could see how big the moose was, and it was *big*. Now he remembered the bumper stickers, t-shirts, and other paraphernalia they'd seen in the gift shops: *Brake for Moose*. He'd assumed they were telling you to slow down so you wouldn't miss *seeing* a moose. Now, gauging the size of the beast that had lumbered into the middle of the road, it occurred to him that the slogan might have meant, "Don't run *into* a moose." The bulk of the moose was in its top half, supported by four spindly legs; in a collision, most of the moose's weight would end up right about where Frank's windshield was, and no airbag in the world was going to save your neck in that situation.

"Why doesn't it move?" Barb asked.

"I don't know." Apparently, moose didn't understand that roads were for cars and that he had the right of way.

The moose took a step toward them, its nostrils flared.

"Frank!" Barb yelled. "It's coming closer."

"I know, I know." He rolled up the windows.

The moose took another step.

"Lock the doors!" Barb yelled.

"What?"

"Lock the doors, lock the doors!"

"Why? You think the moose is gonna try to open a door?"

"Just lock the doors!"

"Awright, awright." He locked the doors and the moose plodded towards them, its nose lowered and sniffing.

Grunt was confused. This didn't look like a female moose. But it had sure sounded like one, making a mating call. The call had stopped—maybe he'd done something to turn her off—but now there was an exotic aroma coming from her feet, or what passed for feet. It wasn't the smell of moose dung but something close, an enticing scent from a distant cousin maybe.

The cow stood stock still, which Grunt took to mean she was at least interested in hearing his pickup lines. He sniffed around, checking out her rear end and underbelly as little squeals of pleasure—at least, he thought it was pleasure, it was hard to tell—came from deep within her.

He moved behind her, his blood pounding now. He rubbed his head along her right flank, then her left, then rested his head along her spine. He gave a little bounce on his front hooves, preparing to mount. A loud cry came from deep within her, and Grunt gave a low growl of pleasure as he hoisted his aging frame up…and came down on empty air. The cow had darted off, moving with amazing speed down that black stretch of earth.

"Wait!" Grunt bellowed. "Come back. We were made for each other!"

Frank looked in the rearview mirror and saw the moose galloping down the road after them. "Son of a—"

"Just drive!" Barb screeched.

He drove. The sky was darkening overhead, and thunder clouds piled up to the west. At this point, Frank's only desire was to get out of Frost Heaves and back to Long Island.

"Turn here," Barb said, studying the map. "There's a cutoff that will take us back to the highway."

A sign at the turn marked Hadley Hill Road, which wound narrowly up, up, and up. At the top of the hill sat an old colonial house with peeling paint and weathered green shutters. It was shaded by a massive maple whose red and orange leaves glowed in the setting sun against the towering thunderclouds. The wind was already whipping up and beginning to shake the leaves off in a colorful shower.

"Stop!" Barb yelled, pointing to the map. "That's the tree!"

"What tree?" Frank said, not slowing down.

"The winner of the contest! The most beautiful tree."

He glanced in the mirror. "Doesn't look that great to me. Let's just get out of here."

She thought about arguing with him, but decided against it. "Fine," she said. There was no disagreeing with him when he got like this.

They passed another old house at the foot of the hill. Homer Cratchet, sitting in his living room, reading the Farm Weekly, heard them when they drove by. Then a flash of lightning exploded outside the house like a giant flashbulb going off. He began counting from one thousand to gauge how far away the lightning had struck. The closer the strike, the sooner the thunder would come. "One thou—" BOOM.

The blast shook the whole house, rattling coffee mugs on the hooks in the kitchen and rearranging the old family photos on the living room wall.

That was close, Homer thought, hoisting himself out of the chair. Then he heard a loud cracking sound like a giant baseball bat knocking one out of the park.

The phone rang and Homer picked it up, carrying the extension to the window to look out. "H'lo?"

"You hear that?" his brother Elmer, who lived a mile away, asked.

"*Hear* it? I felt it in my kidneys."

"Did it land near you?"

"Nope," Homer said, staring up the hill toward Earl Hadley's house. "But it took a big limb off Earl's tree."

"Where'd it land?"

Homer peered out the window. "Looks like it landed in his barn."

"You mean *on* his barn."

"Well, it started out on his barn. Now it's *in* his barn."

"Oh." Elmer was quiet for a moment. "I told him he ought to have that tree trimmed."

"Me, too," Homer said. "But I guess Mother Nature took care of it."

"Ayuh," Elmer said. "Guess so."

WINTER

Happy Holidays, Mostly

Every year, the holiday season kicks off with a Thanksgiving pageant up at the Frost Heaves Community Church. Reverend Woodstead plays the part of Governor Bradford and he tells the story of how the pilgrims came over on the Mayflower and the native Americans saved their necks. The deacons, Sunday school teachers, and kids parade around pretending to plant squash, chop wood, and shoot arrows. The pageant ends up with the whole bunch sitting around a picnic table having Thanksgiving dinner.

This year, Henry Tiffen decided to do something special and brought one of his turkeys to make the pageant more realistic. Henry fed the turkey about a pound of corn to make it dopey and tied a string around its neck to control it. In terms of planning for disaster, this was right up there with the number of lifeboats on the Titanic.

Still, everything was fine until Millard Tuttle drove up to the church in his '57 Chevy International. When Millard shuts his truck off, it backfires, although "backfire" isn't a strong enough word. The sound is somewhere between that of a howitzer firing and Mount St. Helens erupting.

Well, that turkey heard Millard's Chevy and mistook it for a rifle shot, which got him to thinking about his role in this particular production, and he decided he wasn't ready for that level of commitment. Needless to say, the Thanksgiving pageant ended in a kind of a hurry. Also, needless to say, Henry won't be bringing a turkey to the pageant next year.

The weekend after Thanksgiving is always the Snowflake Fair at the church, the highlight of the holiday season, more or less. The members of the Ladies' Guild have been busy for months making crafts to sell, and for once, their meetings have not been marked by the types of squabbles that have happened in the past.

The ladies always have snacks at their craft meetings, and they asked Esther Fernald to bring cider to the first get-together. Esther couldn't find any cider at the Frost Heaves Market, so she went to the MegaMart in Fridley. She didn't find any cider there either till she wandered down the beer aisle and saw some cider that came in 6-packs. She wasn't used to buying cider that way, but she figured it was just as good, so she bought two six-packs.

Back home, she emptied all the bottles into a punch bowl, added a pinch of cinnamon, and brought that to the meeting. Well, the ladies just loved that cider. They asked her to bring it to every meeting, and after that, they got along much better than they used to.

The ladies always come up with elegant crafts. Every year, Millie Tuttle unveils a new design for a knitted toilet paper cover. A few years back, at the time of the royal wedding, she created a set with two dolls knitted up to look like Prince William and Princess Kate. She called it the Royal Flush. This year's design was like a barrel with straps being worn by a man with no clothes on, which was supposed to be a comment about the economy, I guess.

Meanwhile, Mavis Thompkins stunned the crafting competition with Christmas wreaths made out of white plastic shopping bags, which she had cut up and teased out. The wreaths looked kind of furry, like a white cat that's been washed and blow-dried. Mavis got the idea from the craft fair at the Methodist Church in East Mildew. (That's what these women do, they go around to all the other fairs looking for ideas to steal, which is why you see the same things at all the fairs. It's kind of like a virus, or one of them Ponzi schemes.) Anyway, the plastic wreaths weren't a big seller. I guess people weren't ready to trade in their plastic evergreen wreaths yet.

The ladies were also selling copies of their cookbook, *Frost Heavings*. It's pretty good, despite having the world's worst title for a cookbook, and they probably should have had some ground rules before putting the collection together. To begin with, several women submitted meatloaf recipes, but Helen Andrews assumed they would pick her recipe, since she had been bringing her meatloaf to church suppers for twenty years and thinks it is everyone's favorite. The truth is, most folks actually prefer Marjorie Rogers' meatloaf, but no one wanted to tell Helen that. Beatrice Thompkins suggested they simply include both recipes, but then they worried that the other women would wonder why *their* recipes hadn't been included. So the cookbook came out with five recipes for meatloaf, which are all basically the same; we're talking meatloaf here, not Pâté de Foie Grass.

The cookbook also had Bernice Franklin's Carrot Cake. Bernice makes the best carrot cake on the planet.

The problem is, it's a secret recipe and Bernice didn't want to give it away. The women figured they couldn't have a recipe book without Bernice's carrot cake, so they just listed the title and a verse from the Bible, Proverbs 11:13: "A trustworthy man keeps a secret." For church ladies they can be downright sneaky.

Speaking of cake, there's always a lot of baked goods at the Snowflake Fair. Mabel Pillsbury—she fancies herself the Julia Child of Frost Heaves—creates something new every year. This time around, she brought what she called Christmas Surprise cookies, which had cinnamon, ginger, nutmeg, and cayenne pepper. I have to say, they were surprising.

As usual, the ladies had made about twelve kinds of zucchini bread, zucchini relish, zucchini pie, and zucchini I don't-know-what-all. One of the young mothers, Muffy Whittle, even made zucchini quiche, but it didn't go over too well. T'weren't her fault; Muffy is a newcomer, only been in town 12 years, so she didn't know any better.

The other big event right after Thanksgiving is the lighting of the Christmas tree at the town common. That's the Warren Meeker Memorial Tree right next to the gazebo. Warren was a little fella' who lived in town his whole life and took a fair bit of ribbing about his height. When he passed away, he left money in his will for a tree to be planted next to the gazebo. We all thought it was kind of odd, him wanting a tree as a memorial, but no one said anything, him being dead and all.

Warren had requested a specific kind of tree, which was delivered and planted on the common. The label on the tree said "Dawn Redwood," which turns out to be about the fastest-growing tree on the planet. It grows about five feet every year. Right now, it towers over the town, and every year we have to invest in a few more strands of lights to cover the thing. These days, planes flying out of Manchester use it as a landmark. We've thought about taking the tree down, but we decided not to, just in case Santa Claus has as much trouble finding Frost Heaves as everyone else does.

Anyway, we make a big deal of lighting the tree. Everyone gathers around and we sing carols. Then we turn off all the other lights downtown and plug in the tree. We have to, or else it blows all the fuses along Main Street. But it is real pretty, as if all the stars in the sky have drifted down and landed in the tree, brightening up at least one little corner of Frost Heaves.

This year, our local community theatre group put on a performance of the Charles Dickens classic, "A Christmas Carol," which was a highlight of the holiday season. Well, a mid-light, if I'm honest. I've told you about the group, FHART. They are a small group, so they always have to make some adaptations to the script. This year, instead of the ghosts of Christmas Past, Present, and Yet to Come, they had one ghost, the Ghost of Christmas in General. Also, they had a limited budget for props, so Jacob Marley's chains were made out of tin foil. (They had tried using tire chains, but Walter Dunton couldn't make it out of the men's dressing room, let alone rattle the chains.)

The other thing that happens right after Thanksgiving is that the stores in downtown Frost Heaves put out their Christmas displays. They have to wait till then because we passed a warrant article at town meeting years ago that stores couldn't put out Christmas stuff too early. We feel it takes away from the other holidays, like Groundhog Day and Cinco de Mayo.

The merchants call it the Holiday Stroll, with decorations and special items on sale. Of course, there aren't that many stores, so it's a short stroll. Honestly, I do most of my Christmas shopping at the swap shop at the dump, but when I'm looking for a quality item—and understand, I'm using "quality" in a very general sense—I find there are some advantages to shopping in Frost Heaves.

First of all, at those big box stores, you always have to fight your way through the crowds at Christmas time. But in Frost Heaves, you are never bothered by a lot of other shoppers. Nor will you be pestered by a gaggle of salespeople asking if they can help you. In fact, you may have to holler to rouse someone. But once you do, you'll have the complete personal attention of a sales clerk who doesn't really have anything else to do. And you're sure to be treated as if you were their only customer—because you may be.

Personally, I started the Holiday Stroll at the market, where Moochie was grinding up venison for his reindeer burgers, always a hit this time of year. He also put together some gift baskets of Perfectly Good products. These are items that are just a little past their sell-by date, but they're still perfectly good. He puts them in gift baskets that he finds at the swap shop—Louise saves them for him—and he decorates the baskets with candy canes—also left over from last year or the year before— which you can use to decorate your Christmas tree, or eat them if your teeth are up for the challenge.

Over at the Bait 'n' Beauty Shoppe, Rhonda Lafleur had a special going called, "All I Want for Christmas is Some Night Crawlers and a Perm." She was also offering 50% off her Kindalike beauty supplies, a line of knockoff products she developed herself: Kindalike Vidal Sassoon, Kindalike Clairol, Kindalike Paul Mitchell, and so on. She won't say what's in them, but to me, most of them smell kind of like laundry soap.

Next, I wandered over to Dingle's Hardware Store, where Charlie had brought in some real nice items for Christmas, including a square egg maker. You put in a boiled egg and squeeze, and it comes out square. It's amazing what modern technology can do. I got one of them for the missus, so don't say nothing if you see her.

Charlie also had earrings made out of little No-Pest strips—those should come in real handy during black fly season—and something for the home handyman called the Fix-It-All Repair Kit, with everything you need to fix just about anything in your home. I'll let you in on a secret: inside the box is just a roll of duct tape.

Charlie also stocks some of those good old-fashioned products you can't find anymore, like Fels-Naptha soap, Bon Ami cleanser, Beaman's Gum, and Pine-Tar Shampoo. These are the actual, original items, not reproductions—Charlie's got a cellar full of 'em. True, they're a bit dusty and way past their sell-by dates, but I bet they're just as good as the day they was made, mostly.

After a busy morning of window shopping, I was feeling peckish, so I stopped by the Bluebell Diner, where Bud was whipping up his special Christmas wreath pastries. These are basically just cinnamon rolls, except they're the size of a Christmas wreath, so you need a lot of coffee to go with 'em. Speaking of which, Bud just cleaned the coffee pot at the diner, so the coffee should be pretty fresh for a while. A few of the locals are ticked off about this, they claim the coffee doesn't taste the same, which is probably true. Some of these folks would drink battery acid if you put enough cream in it.

Over at the Frost Heaves House of Pizza, chef Walter Dunton was whipping up a special he calls the Advent Pizza, with four sections: Love, Joy, Peace, and Pepperoni. Wouldn't that add a festive touch to your Christmas table? Plus, it comes with an order of fries.

To finish up the stroll, I got in the car and headed to Herb Cullen's farm stand. Herb always gets in a load of bargain Christmas trees, trees that stood out in the field too long and are too big for most homes. But Herb says if you cut the top off, they still look fine. The price varies, depending on whether you want the top or the bottom.

For the gardeners on your shopping list, Herb has Christmas tins filled with Garden Marvel fertilizer. This is 100% post-bovine organic fertilizer, guaranteed to make your poinsettia grow like a house afire. And you get the reusable Christmas tin, though you might want to sterilize it before you put cookies in it. Herb was selling the Garden Marvel tins for a buck apiece, but people didn't seem that interested. Then he put up a sign that said, "Deal of the Week, 3 for $5." Now they're flying off the shelf, which tells you something about the Frost Heaves educational system.

Personally, I think I'll stick to Christmas shopping at the swap shop. The price is right, returns are simple, and the products have stood the test of time. A long time.

NEWS NUGGETS:
Road report

If you have been out on the roads at all, you know it's a bad year for frost heaves. It's like a roller coaster on some of the back roads. One female resident, who shall not be named, broke down and bought her first sports bra.

As a result, the highway department has begun its annual used auto parts sale. The guys have a fine assortment of mufflers, hubcaps, and bumpers, as well as a selection of hats, mittens, and other winter apparel. Stop by and check out the goods. All proceeds will go to buying a new coffee pot for the town garage, and if you've tasted the coffee there, you know why.

Clarence's Cookies

The missus and I got our first Christmas card the other day:

Wishing you all the joys of the season. Hope to see you soon.

Of course, that was from the funeral home.

Back in the day, we used to get hundreds of Christmas cards. It got to be so the missus would open a card and read, "Merry Christmas from the Flendermans."

"Who are the Flendermans?" I'd ask.

"I don't know," she'd say. "But we'd better send them a card. I don't want them to think we don't like them."

It is also party season and lots of folks are having get-togethers. Last weekend, the guys at Bundy's garage had their annual Christmas party. Bundy loads up his old soda machine with beer, and Doreen puts out a spread for the guys. They have a great time, eating and singing Christmas carols. Bundy owns the loudspeaker that the town uses for the winter carnival, and after the guys have had a few drinks, they'll usually set up the system so the town can hear how good their singing is—a matter of opinion, to say the least. As the evening progresses and their imbibing continues, they start to substitute new words for the originals. By the time they got to "O, Little Town of Bethlehem," it came out like this.

"O, little town of Frost Heaves,
how still we see thee lie.
If folks knew what a dump you were,
they'd surely pass you by."

On the other side of town, my old teacher Beatrice Thompkins was having a kind of blue Christmas. She has taught school in Frost Heaves longer than it takes most fossils to form. Just about everyone in town had Miss Thompkins as their teacher at one time or another.

But these days, Beatrice feels kind of wore out. After all those years, you'd think teaching would get easier, but it just seems to get harder. And lately, she had been wondering if it was all worth it.

She was getting ready for the holiday party at the school and she hates having to call it a holiday party. She is old school, she's got nothing against those other holidays, she just thinks if you're celebrating Christmas, you should call it Christmas.

She feels the same way about Christmas gift wrap. These days, you can find gift wrap with Santa Claus, reindeer, snowmen, Christmas trees, and your favorite cartoon characters. But good luck finding wrapping paper with the baby Jesus, or wise men, or even angels. To Beatrice, this is like having a birthday party where the birthday boy isn't even invited.

Beatrice is also upset about the passing of Christmas cards. She used to get a hundred cards, many from her old students, and she always looked forward to hearing what they were up to. But these days, people can't be bothered, and that discourages her too. So far, Beatrice had gotten about a dozen Christmas cards, and she had taken to parceling them out to make them last longer.

That particular day, she had only gotten one card, which she saved until after supper. She sat in her chair and picked up the card, glanced at the return address, and gave a little gasp. The address read "Walters," and that was a name she had not heard in 25 years.

The Walters family had lived on the other side of the tracks in Frost Heaves—literally—in a dilapidated old railroad building that looked as if the next train to pass by would blow it down. Fortunately for the Walters, no trains had passed through Frost Heaves since 1938, when the Great Hurricane took out the railroad bridge.

The Walters children—and there were a number of them—wore ragged hand-me-downs. Their mother cut their hair using a bowl that she stuck on top of their heads, and their shoes were passed down from one kid to the next until they fell apart. Needless to say, the other kids in town tended to pick on the Walters brood, especially their youngest boy, Clarence. You hear a lot about bullying these days, but it isn't anything new. Clarence was the target of a lot of meanness back then.

Holding that card, Beatrice remembered a Christmas when she had asked her students for volunteers to make cookies for the Christmas party. She was actually asking the kids to volunteer their mothers to make cookies. Teachers can be sneaky when they have to.

Right away, Clarence Walters shot his hand up, "Me, me! Let me."

Beatrice ignored him because she knew that Mrs. Walters struggled to make ends meet and didn't have money for extras like cookies.

But Clarence kept it up, and Beatrice knew that if she didn't let him bring cookies, his feelings would be hurt—and Clarence's feelings had already been hurt too many times in his young life. Besides, only a few other children had volunteered their mothers' services, so she told him OK.

The day of the Christmas party, Clarence marched into school with a plate of homemade cookies. Beatrice took the plate and said, "Thank you, Clarence. These look very nice."

"I made them myself," Clarence said, beaming.

Beatrice got a little pale. "You did?"

"Uh-huh. And I never made cookies before, either."

Beatrice took a closer look at the cookies and figured Clarence was telling the truth. Among other things in the lumpy brown nuggets, she could make out bits of unmixed baking powder, some unidentified nuts, and a few other ingredients she wasn't sure about. Well, she thought, children will eat anything if it's a cookie. Maybe these weren't that bad. She put the cookies on the snack table and hoped for the best.

By the time the party rolled around, however, word had gotten out: those funny-looking cookies down at the end had been made by Clarence Walters. There was no way the other kids were going to eat those cookies. According to the kid code of conduct, you could get cooties merely by *sitting* next to Clarence, let alone eating a cookie that he made. So Clarence's cookies sat on the table, unwanted and uneaten, while the other cookies disappeared. And Clarence's eyes slowly filled with tears.

Beatrice saw what was happening, and she knew what she had to do. She waited until Clarence was watching, then she picked up one of those cookies and closed her eyes for a moment. She was thinking about a place in the Bible where Jesus said, "As much as you have done it unto one of the least of these my brethren, you have done it unto me." She was also remembering the time he said that his followers would eat poison and it wouldn't hurt them. "Lord," she prayed, "I'm doing this for this little boy here. Please don't let it kill me."

That cookie was probably the worst thing Beatrice had ever eaten in her entire life. But she gave Clarence a weak smile, and said, "Mm…very nice." Which wasn't a lie—they had *looked* nice.

Clarence was thrilled. "Do you want another one?"

Beatrice took a deep breath. Clearly, no one else was going to eat any of Clarence's cookies. "Why yes, Clarence."

Eating that first cookie had been a test of faith. The second one was pure courage. Beatrice choked it down and then asked Clarence if she could take the rest of them home with her. She didn't say what she was going to do with them when she got them home, but Clarence was happy anyway.

The next year, the Walters family moved away, and Beatrice never heard from them again. Until now, 25 years later. She opened the envelope, and inside was a Christmas card with a nativity scene on the front and a note inside.

Dear Miss Thompkins,

You probably don't remember me, but you were my teacher for one year when we lived in Frost Heaves. We moved away after that and I never kept in touch with anyone from town, but I will never forget you. You were very kind to me when I was young.

Last week in church, our minister was preaching about thankfulness, and she challenged us to think about people we are grateful for, people who might have made a difference in our lives. She said we should be sure to let those people know. So I just wanted to thank you for encouraging me when I really needed it.

I hope all is well with you. Merry Christmas and best wishes,
Clarence Walters

Enclosed with the card was a photograph of a young couple standing outside a diner with two small children. On the back of the photo was a note. "This is my wife Diana and I with our kids Heather and Jack, in front of our diner, which we bought after I graduated from culinary school. We call it the High Hopes Diner.

By this time, Beatrice was having a hard time reading because her eyes were leaking. From down the street, she could hear the guys at the garage singing. They were starting to wind down, pretty well lubricated at this point, but they managed to get out one last carol without messing it up.

"How silently, how silently, the wondrous gift is given.
So God imparts to human hearts the blessings of his heaven.
No ear may hear his coming, but in this world of sin,
where meek souls will receive him still,
the dear Christ enters in."

Police Log: Shots Fired

On Friday, Officer Lamott responded to reports of shots fired on Upper Fridley Road. Upon investigation, he determined that the shots had come from the home of Arthur Bascom. When Lamott knocked, Bascom opened the door holding a shotgun and said, "What's up?"

"We got a report of shots being fired," Lamott said.

"Ayuh," Bascom responded. "I got a squirrel in my house. Trying to get him."

Lamott noted that the house showed much evidence of Bascom having failed to get the squirrel so far, but decided to leave him to it. "I guess if he wants to shoot up his own house, that's up to him," Lamott stated.

Merry Christmas, Millard Tuttle

Up to the Frost Heaves Community Church, the handbell choir has begun practicing for the Christmas Eve service. The handbell choir is a bunch of older folks under the direction of Dottie McPhee, the choir director. They call themselves the Rolling Tones—not to be confused with that other group, although they are about the same age.

If you've never seen a handbell choir, it's quite something. Instead of having one person play an instrument, the music is broken up amongst 8 or 10 people, each of whom has just two notes to play. This takes a fair bit of coordination, more than the Rolling Tones actually have, unfortunately.

To begin with, most of them cannot read music, so they have to watch Dottie to see when she points to them. They also don't see very well and when they realize she's pointing to them, it's too late, but then they play anyway. (You don't get many notes when the music is broken up like that, and you don't want to miss any.) As a result, the handbell choir generally sounds like a bunch of musical bees swarming in the general direction of the melody.

The other special music for Christmas Eve will be Mavis Thompkins. I've told you about Mavis, her singing will remove tarnish from silverware. She has been working up a special number, "O Holy Night," and when she sings the high part of the song, "fall on your knees," you really want to.

This year, our organist Sophie Hamilton has a new piece of equipment that she's pretty tickled about, a clip-on light over her music stand. The deacons approved this purchase so that we don't have the same problem we had last year on Christmas Eve. When people showed up for the service, we handed each one a little white candle. Then, at the end of the service, we turned off all the lights except for one big candle on the altar. The idea was for the ushers to light their candles from the big one, then light the candles of the people in the pews, passing the light from one person to another while we all sang "Silent Night."

It didn't work out so well. When the lights went out, we all stood in the dark, waiting for Sophie to start playing "Silent Night," but nothing happened. This went on for quite a while until Sophie hollered, "I can't see!"

Nobody knew what to do at that point, so Sophie started playing a song she knew by heart, one she had taught hundreds of piano students over the years: "Twinkle, Twinkle, Little Star." That wasn't exactly what we had planned for Christmas Eve, although it was quite moving.

The week before Christmas, the Frost Heaves Community Church always does a live nativity scene out in front of the church. We used to have plywood cutouts for Joseph, Mary, and the other characters, but someone suggested we should have real people play the parts, so that's what we've done for the past few years. The jury is still out on whether the plywood figures or the live folks put on a better show.

The cast members dress up in their bathrobes, with towels tied around their heads and Velcro sandals. This year, Maudie Perkins offered to bring her pet sheep to be part of the tableau as well. That sounded like a good idea until word got out that Maudie was bringing her pet, and pretty soon, everybody else wanted to bring their pets as well. So instead of donkeys and camels adoring the baby Jesus, we had half a dozen cats, two poodles, one pit bull, a hamster, and a goldfish. That was OK until Helen Andrew's poodle Mitzi lifted her leg against the back of the stable. When you're trying to look all holy and angelic, there's nothing like poodle pee to ruin the mood. If you remember the story, Mary and Joseph took off for Egypt right after Jesus was born, and in this case, the Holy Family decided to get an early start and beat the traffic. Needless to say, we have banned pets from all future productions.

The other thing that was different about the live nativity this year was the baby Jesus. We always have the newest baby in town play the part of Jesus, but folks kind of fell down on the job last year, and the part was played by Elsa Franklin's baby doll Leroy, who was surprisingly good in the role.

This year, so as not to repeat that problem, we put a notice in the paper in February to remind the young couples in town that we would be needing a baby for the live nativity and that they should get to work. They really took that to heart and we ended up with several candidates for the part, so to make things fair, we decided to use all of the babies and swap them out of the nativity every so often.

The other big holiday event this week was the cookie sale at the church. The way it works, each of the women in the church bakes a couple dozen of her favorite cookies and takes them to the church for the sale. Then they buy cookies from the other women and bring them home.

To their husbands, this don't make a lot of sense. You start off with a batch of cookies that you like, and you end up with a bunch of strange cookies that may or may not be any good—and you pay for the privilege.

Millard Tuttle was particularly ticked off about the cookie sale. His wife, Millie, makes the best sugar cookies in New Hampshire, and they are always a favorite at the cookie sale. Nobody knows how she does it, but those sugar cookies just melt in your mouth. Honest, they are a little bit of heaven on earth. Millard loves those sugar cookies and it was torture for him, being in a house where sugar cookies were being made, knowing that he was not going to get any and that they were all headed for the cookie sale.

The other thing that Millard was ticked off about was not being asked to play Santa Claus this year at the church Christmas party. Millard has played Santa for years, but last year a few of the kids told their parents Santa smelled funny—like sour fruit, they said—which was probably because he had stopped off at the Peabody Tavern for a little Christmas cheer before the party.

Word of this got back to the church ladies, and they decided to hire a professional Santa this year, someone from away with an actual beard and a nice Santa costume instead of the fake cotton beard and moth-eaten outfit that Millard always wore.

Millard didn't say nothing, but his feelings were hurt. Then came the cookie sale, adding sugar-dusted insult to injury. When Millie made all those cookies and headed to the church to drop them off without offering him a single one, it was just too much. He stomped out of the house and didn't even leave a note about where he was going.

Millie came back from church and started cleaning up. Her cat Dolly was hanging around begging, so Millie scraped the cookie bowl and offered her the leftovers. Dolly took one sniff and walked away, which had never happened before, and that made Millie wonder what was going on.

She tasted the dough herself, and it was the saltiest thing she had ever eaten. Then she realized what she had done. She had mixed up her baking jars and instead of a cup of sugar, she had put a cup of salt in those cookies.

She raced back to the church to get the cookies before anyone bought them, but it was too late. Somebody had already snapped them up.

Needless to say, Millie was beside herself. Her reputation as a good cook had narrowly escaped the Great Meatloaf Disaster of the previous year, but when word of this got out, her culinary career would be over. She went home and spent the rest of that day fretting about it.

The other person who was fretting that day was the new Santa Claus that the church ladies had hired. He hadn't asked for directions to Frost Heaves because he had one of them GPS devices and he figured that would get him there, which was a bad assumption. He had driven all over the county and he was no closer to Frost Heaves than when he started. The GPS kept harping at him, and pretty soon he and the GPS were bickering at each other to the point where he just turned it off.

Meanwhile, Millard Tuttle had been out wassailing. Wassailing is where you go from house to house singing Christmas carols until they invite you in for a drink of wassail or whatever else they might have on hand. Millard had hit a number of houses and the Christmas carols—like Millard—were getting looser and looser. In fact, to the casual observer, it probably looked as if Millard was just standing outside of people's houses yelling, but those folks all knew Millard, so they invited him in for a drink anyway.

As twilight came on, Millard arrived at the end of Main Street by the church and found a tiny house where people in party clothes were standing around staring at a baby. It was an odd bunch—no matter how loud Millard sang, they didn't invite him in for a drink. And despite the fact that they were all staring at the baby, none of 'em seemed to notice when someone came in, took the kid and left another one in its place.

Even in his less-than-fully-lucid state, Millard knew this was wrong. He spun around and tottered off towards the police station to report the kidnapping, but by the time he got there he'd forgotten why, so he just headed home.

By now, the stars were beginning to come out, and despite the cold it was a beautiful evening. About halfway down Lazybrook Road, Millard came upon an old Honda Civic pulled over to the side of the road. He walked up to the car and saw the person behind the wheel studying a map, so he tapped on the window to see if he could help.

The driver jumped up, startled, but not as startled as Millard, because the driver was Santa Claus. Millard was kind of surprised to see him driving a Honda Civic, he always pictured Santa as more of a Chevy Impala kind of guy.

"Help you?" he asked.

Santa looked embarrassed. "Can you tell me how to get to Frost Heaves?"

Several wiseacre responses occurred to Millard, not the least of which was our town motto, "You can't get there from here." But he realized pretty quick that if this guy didn't know where Frost Heaves was, he wasn't the real Santa, just a fill-in. In fact, he was probably the guy who had taken away Millard's job. It would serve the guy right if Millard simply said, "I don't know."

But then Millard looked up at the twilight sky, and there was a single bright star blazing away high up above the trees. It was so beautiful, it reminded him of the Bethlehem star. That got him to thinking about Christmas, which made him think about all those little kids waiting up at the church for Santa Claus to arrive.

So Millard made up his mind. He gave the guy directions to town—by this time he was sobering up enough to remember them—and slapped the roof of the car as he said, "Giddyup."

Unfortunately, Santa had got himself into a rut, and the wheels started to spin. He gunned it, but the wheels just spun more. Millard tried to give the car a shove, to no avail. He looked around for something to throw under the tires for traction, but he couldn't find anything.

It was getting cold, so he stuck his hands in his pockets, and that's when he felt Millie's sugar cookies. He had bought them at the cookie sale, all two dozen of them, and he had been saving them until he got home. He had planned to eat every single one by himself and not offer them to anybody else.

But then he looked up at that star again, and it was so beautiful, as if God had hung it up there just for him. And it struck him that a lot of times in life, we don't get what we deserve. Despite all the pain and disappointment life may bring, we also get so many beautiful things that we haven't done a thing to earn: love, forgiveness, blueberries on a sunny hilltop, a single star hanging in a twilight sky.

At that point, Millard made one of the toughest decisions of his life. Despite how much he loved those sugar cookies, he started chucking them under the wheels of that Civic, every last one of them. Santa gave it the gas, and right away the wheels grabbed hold. Millard was kind of surprised at how well those cookies provided traction, like a Christmas miracle. The Civic pulled away and Santa headed off with a toot of his horn.

Meanwhile, back at the Tuttle place, Millie was feeling bad that she hadn't made any sugar cookies for her husband of 50-odd years. She was wondering if maybe the incident with the first batch was a message to her about pride. So she made a fresh batch of cookies—the right way this time—just for him.

Millard didn't know that, of course. He was just walking home, looking up at that star and singing that beautiful old Christmas carol.

"Twinkle, Twinkle, little star…"

NEWS NUGGETS:
Millie's Sugar Cookies

Millie Tuttle has provided us with her famous sugar cookie recipe, complete with her notes.

Ingredients: ¾ cup butter (Don't use shortening or margarine. I don't care what they say, it isn't the same.)
1 cup sugar
2 eggs (make sure they're fresh, not the ones that have been sitting in the back of the fridge for a month)
1 tsp vanilla
2 ½ cups flour
1 tsp baking powder
1 tsp salt

Mix the first four ingredients together. In a separate bowl, mix the dry ingredients. Blend them into the butter mixture a little at a time. Chill for one hour, and don't cut that short just because you're in an all-fired rush. Roll out the dough and cut with cookie cutters. Place on ungreased sheet. Bake at 400 degrees for 6 to 8 minutes and for goodness' sake whatever you do, don't overbake them. If you do, don't blame me.

Perfect Gifts

L ast weekend was the Christmas pageant up at the Frost Heaves Community Church. As always, the littlest kids played the part of the sheep, which they hate, and I can't say as I blame 'em. Kids have been wearing those sheep costumes since the Civil War, and by now they smell like actual sheep, especially when the humidity is high. Let's just say the kids can't wait to graduate to the angel choir.

Speaking of the angel choir, it's a "no-cuts" group, which means everyone gets to sing, including the good, the bad, and those who couldn't carry a tune if it was duct-taped to their bodies.

The kids doing the readings for the pageant were of different heights, and each one adjusted the microphone to suit themselves, so each scripture began with a god-awful screech that woke up even the sleepiest audience member.

The boy playing the innkeeper was chewing gum ambitiously while delivering his lines. "Sorry…chomp, chomp…We're full up…chomp, chomp…There's no room at the inn…chomp, chomp." When he was done, he moved the microphone forward. As the curtain closed on the scene, it knocked over the mic, which hit the floor with a deafening thud like someone had dropped a refrigerator on the roof, again startling those who had almost managed to drift off.

There are always one or two adults taking part in the pageant. This year, Clara Franklin played the part of prophet Anna, an old lady who hung out at the temple in Jerusalem. According to the Bible, when Jesus's folks brought him to the Temple, Anna prophesied over him and said he was going to be something special.

The problem is, Clara is getting up there, and let's just say her tray table isn't always in the upright and locked position. When Mary and Joseph showed up with the baby Jesus, Clara was supposed to sing, "What Child Is This?" Instead, she just stared at him for a long while, knowing she was supposed to do something but not sure what. Then it came to her—she was supposed to sing. So she did, belting out "You Are My Sunshine," which isn't the worst mistake anyone's ever made, I guess.

Clara recently moved into a senior residence in Frost Heaves called Shady Haven. It's an older establishment, not like one of your fancy senior living places with fine dining options and field trips to art museums. Shady Haven is just a bunch of old folks who are better off living together than on their own, arguing over which game show to watch on the TV in the common room. I describe it as an assorted living facility.

Clara did not really want to move there, but her husband Russell passed away a few years back and she had been living by herself till her daughter Marie convinced her it was time to move to Shady Haven. Marie has done everything she can to make things comfortable for Clara, fixing up her room with all her own stuff to make it feel like home.

The room has an old, unused fireplace, and Marie put some of Clara's favorite knickknacks and family photos on the mantel. Right in the middle is Clara's beloved mantel clock, an ornate antique affair with marble on the top and bottom and little columns on either side, which Russell gave to her years ago. That clock sat on the mantel of Clara's home the whole time Marie was growing up. To her, it represents the perfect gift. It was something her mother wanted, it was impractical, a little expensive, and it took some thought and effort on her father's part to get it.

Marie is married to Dave Miller, who is an engineer and a little handicapped in the gift area. Like a lot of men, he has no idea how to buy presents for women. It isn't that they don't care, they just don't get it. For example, most men like tools, so they figure women will appreciate something that will help them out around the house, something practical—an iron, a new hose for the garden. Here's a clue, men: if it's practical, she don't want it. She wants something impractical, something romantic.

The smart women have learned to help the men out. Of course, sometimes they go overboard. For example, Marie has been hinting about wanting to go to Paris for years. (I mean Paris, France, not Paris, Maine, which is a place she might actually get to someday.) You can't just spring something like that on a guy sudden like, you got to work up to it. Maybe start by asking for a sweater or a piece of jewelry.

Anyway, over the years Dave has given Marie some truly horrible gifts, which I will not go into for fear of embarrassing anybody. You might be reading this and be the victim (or perpetrator) of similar gifts, and I don't want to bring up painful memories.

Of course, Marie also finds it almost impossible to buy presents for Dave. Not for want of trying, men are just hard to buy presents for. I don't know why that is. Every year, Marie asks Dave what he wants for Christmas and he says, "I don't know. I don't need anything." But you know who would be upset if there weren't anything under the tree for him, don't you?

Just last week, Marie was at the town office paying their taxes and she got to complaining about this to Edith Wyer, our town clerk. I've told you about Edith, she knows everything about everybody who was married, buried, baptized, downsized, or anaesthetized in Frost Heaves in the past 75 years.

Marie was telling Edith that she didn't know what to get Dave for Christmas. Now, this was outside Edith's normal field of investigative operations, but she took it as a personal challenge. That same day, she started snooping around, talking to folks at the dump, the garage, and the fire station where Dave is a volunteer. The only info she came up with was that Dave had blocked off a couple of weeks in April on the fire station schedule, which the guys couldn't understand. Dave hardly ever takes a vacation, and when he does he mostly just stays around town, so they didn't know what was up.

Then, during choir practice up to the church, Edith was chatting with Bertha Eldridge and she hit pay dirt, gossip-wise. As it happens, the choir was practicing "I Love to Tell the Story," which seems fitting. Bertha whispered to Edith, "I probably shouldn't say anything, but Dave Miller has been spending a lot of time over at the widow LaVeuve's apartment."

Francine LaVeuve is 32, blonde, and she's got a figure that gives men neck spasms when she walks down the street. She lives in an apartment on Main Street and as it happens, Edith's daughter and her family live in the apartment above Francine. There is a heating duct that connects the two, which Edith just happened to know acts like a speaker system—that house used to belong to her grandparents, and she spent many a happy hour as a youngster listening at the vent, honing her emerging talent for gossip gathering.

Edith offered to babysit for her daughter's kids that Friday, and her daughter BeeBee and son-in-law headed over to East Mildew to go bowling. (BeeBee's real name is Barbara, but no one calls her that. Here in New England, we seem to have a propensity for giving people odd names based on something they did or said when they were youngsters or a sibling's inability to pronounce their names. So you have DeeDee, Dit, Weensie, Deetsie, Peetsie, and the like. And in BeeBee's case, she was just as glad to ditch the name Barb Wyer when she married Tom Platt, for obvious reasons.)

Anyway, as soon as BeeBee and Tom headed out, Edith fed the kids, put them to bed, and planted herself next to the heating duct. Sure enough, pretty soon she started to hear words of torrid romance—in French, no less—coming up from the widow LaVeuve's apartment.

First, Francine said something that sounded like, "Qu'est-ce qu'il y a à manger?"

Then Dave said, very slowly, "Des saucisses, sans doute."

"Qu'est-ce qui est arrivé?" Francine asked.

"Tu vois bien, je suis tombé," Dave responded.

Edith had no idea what that all meant, but she was sure they were words of passion and she had heard enough. This was scandalous, the juiciest gossip ever. But now she had a dilemma. She couldn't bear to keep this to herself, but she knew that once it hit the grapevine, it was going to ruin Marie's life. After a while though, she decided that somebody needed to tell Marie, like it or not.

As it happens, Marie came to the town office the next day to pay her water bill. After the usual pleasantries, Edith took a deep breath and said, "Do you know the widow LaVeuve?"

"Francine?" Marie said. "She's my best friend."

Edith took another deep breath, but before she could say anything, Marie said, "That poor girl. She's been having such a hard time since her husband passed away. She started giving French lessons just to make ends meet. I even tried to get Dave to take lessons on the outside chance that we ever go to Paris. But he said no."

Then Edith remembered about the time off that Dave was planning in April. And now that she thought about it, the conversation she'd overheard between Dave and Francine sounded vaguely familiar, like something from way back in 7th-grade French class. And suddenly it all clicked.

"So what about Francine?" Marie said.

"Oh, never mind," Edith said, turning back to Marie's water bill to change the subject. She handed Marie the receipt and said, "By the way, I know what you can get Dave for Christmas. A suitcase."

"Why?"

Edith shrugged. "Every man should have a good suitcase. And if he doesn't like it, he can exchange it for something else."

Marie was considering that when her cell phone rang, as it did at least eight times a day. "That's Mom," she said, glancing at the phone. "I'd better go."

Standing on the steps of the town hall, she said, "What is it, Mom?"

"What channel is my show on?" Clara asked.

"What show?"

"You know, that cooking show."

"I told you, channel 121, the same as it has always been."

"Oh. OK." Clara hung up, put on her sweater, and then forgot that she was going to watch TV. So she sat down and looked up at her mantel clock, reminiscing about Christmases past. Her memory wasn't that good, but she remembered the Christmas when she got that clock as if it were yesterday.

After the kids had opened all their presents, Russell handed her a heavy package, which he had clearly wrapped himself—overlapping edges, too much tape, a cockeyed bow. But he had a look on his face like a little boy giving a present to his mother. The kids watched as Clara opened it up, sly grins and wide eyes as if they knew what it was.

It was the mantel clock. Clara looked at it kind of funny. "Isn't that something?" she said noncommittally. "Where did you get it?"

"Don't you remember?" Russell said. "We were in that antique shop in Kittery, and you saw this clock and said how much you liked it."

"Oh, that's right. Thank you, dear. It's lovely."

What Clara didn't tell Russell was that the clock she liked had been the one *next* to this clock at the antique shop. That one was a little ceramic clock with porcelain roses twisted around the face of the dial. She had pointed it out to Russell, but he must have thought she meant the one next to it.

The clock Russell bought was perhaps the ugliest thing Clara had ever seen. But she put it up on their mantel, and it stayed there for the next 27 years. She never told Russell, never told her kids, never told anyone. Because as much as she disliked that clock, she loved Russell, loved the fact that he had gone all the way back to that store in Maine and spent a fair bit of money just to get something he thought she wanted. It didn't matter that it was the wrong clock. To her, that clock was the perfect gift, because it reminded her of his love for her. And money can't buy that kind of love.

So Clara sat in her rocker, looking at the clock and singing softly to herself. "You are my sunshine, my only sunshine…"

NEWS NUGGETS:
Swap Shop Christmas

Once again, the swap shop at the dump will be open for last-minute shoppers on Christmas Eve. Get there early, because on Christmas Eve, the good stuff goes fast. This year, members of the Loon Lodge will be gift wrapping any item from the swap shop for a small donation to the food bank. For wrapping paper, they'll be using leftover wallpaper donated by Helen Andrews, who had been keeping it for years in case she needed to repair a rip or tear. This is industrial-strength wrapping paper and the guys expect to be doing a brisk business, but be forewarned. It's cold out there, and they keep a flask of Bert Woodbury's maple spirits to ward off the chill. Let's just say that if you show up late in the afternoon, you will not be getting their best work.

Unexpected Christmas

The choir went out caroling along Main Street this week, and as usual, a lot of folks pretended they weren't home. The choir tried something new this year, they brought along the handbells to play. That would have been fine, except there was a light freezing rain, then it turned bitter cold and the clappers froze. Imagine a group of mimes playing Silent Night and you'll get the picture. It's no wonder Millard Tuttle calls them the Moron Tabernacle Choir. Still, the choir was excited because there was a photographer in town and he took their picture, which got in the paper.

Pastor Woodstead was up at the church, working on his Christmas sermon. It's never easy to give a meaningful sermon on Christmas Eve, knowing that you're fighting a losing battle against the presents that still have to be wrapped, the turkey that didn't get thawed in time, and the sheets that have to be washed for the guest bed.

He was planning to call his sermon "Come, Thou Unexpected Jesus." His idea was that Jesus's birth wasn't what anyone would have expected. You would think that if God was going to show up, he'd be pretty dramatic about it, like a king riding into town on a war horse to free the people from Roman oppression, not a baby born in a stable.

To help people relate to the Christmas story better, he thought he might try telling it as if Jesus had been born in Frost Heaves: "And lo, there were ice fishermen watching over their lines by night. And suddenly, a bright light shone round about them, and it was Agnes Deo, part-time police officer, in the cruiser with the spotlight on. She was coming to get old Doc Shepherd, because a baby had just been born in town."

He would continue with the fishermen coming into town to look for the baby. "And they found the baby wrapped in a plaid flannel shirt, lying in a toolbox in the garage of Betty Haskell's B&B, because the place was full up, what with it being Christmas week and all."

When the wise men showed up, they would bring gifts of beans, chowder, and maple syrup. Since he was setting the story in Frost Heaves, he was having a hard time coming up with wise men. Wise guys we have, but wise men, not so much. Then it occurred to him that the actual wise men were dignitaries from faraway places, so maybe they'd be presidential candidates—although he thinks anybody who actually wants to be president isn't wise but crazy and ought to be locked up.

Pastor Woodstead probably had candidates on his mind because Senator Edwin Quagmire stopped by Frost Heaves this week. Senator Quagmire is running for president with the campaign slogan, "The lesser of quite a few evils." Formerly Commissioner of Mattress Safety for Idaho, he has been described by those who know him as "short." He is the only politician we got to take us up on our NOPE package, which tells you something about how desperate he was.

Senator Quagmire had been at a lunch meeting in Manchester with what he assumed was the New Hampshire Association of Extremely Loud People, each of whom had been given a bag of potato chips with their lunch, which they proceeded to chomp noisily while he was speaking.

After the meeting, he headed over to Vermont. His driver was a young man from his home state of Idaho, where the land is flat and the roads are straight. When you learn to drive in a place like that and come to New England, with its convoluted roads and highways, it's like asking someone to take the controls of a fighter jet when their only previous experience is one of them kiddie plane rides outside the supermarket. That young driver was depending on his GPS, which as I've mentioned is always a mistake around here. (Bundy, who runs the local garage, says that the GPS is the best thing to happen to tow truck drivers since the invention of beer.)

At any rate, the senator and his driver got lost. They pulled over, the driver rummaged in the glove compartment, and he found an actual paper map. (Depending on your age, you might be surprised to learn that maps actually used to be printed on large sheets of paper. You had to find your own way from point A to point B, which some people were better at than others. The story goes that Columbus only bumped into the New World because he was bad at folding maps and had misread his.)

So there the senator was, stuck on the side of the road. Cars and trucks drove by, staring at this big, black rental car with Massachusetts plates, but nobody stopped to see if things were OK. This made the senator feel as if he were in a foreign country, which he was. If this had happened in Idaho, by now they would have had four offers of help and two invitations to come for dinner and meet the folks. But this is New England; we don't like to bother anyone and we don't like to be bothered.

Eventually, the senator and his driver made it to Frost Heaves. It was getting late, so they decided to stay at the Peabody Inn, which is not exactly the Ritz-Carlton. To begin with, the inn does not have private bathrooms, you have to share a bathroom down at the end of the hall.

That was fine with the senator until about ten o'clock when he had to pee in a hurry, at which point he realized he hadn't brought a robe with him. He peeked out the door and didn't see anyone, so he just scooted down the hall in his birthday suit.

Just as he was finishing his business, he heard two people meeting in the hallway. He waited for them to finish their conversation and move on, but it turned out that these were old friends who hadn't seen each other in years, and they had a fair bit of catching up to do.

So the senator sat there, reading every joke in the last dozen issues of Reader's Digest, waiting for the party to break up. The confab didn't show any signs of ending soon, so he began examining his options.

There were no towels in the bathroom, no rug he could wrap around himself. He looked out the window at the roof over the porch that ran along the front of the inn. He figured if worse came to worst, he could crawl out the window and along the roof to his room. There aren't any street lights in front of the inn, so he figured no one would see him.

Looking out the window and pondering this option, he noticed the house across the street, where a young woman in an upstairs bedroom was putting her kids to bed.

That was Annie Wilson. Her husband Henry is serving overseas, his third tour, so she is essentially a single mom this Christmas. She has two little girls, and it has been hard on them having their daddy away. But Annie was determined to make this the best Christmas they had ever had.

The day after Thanksgiving, she decorated the house top to bottom. She even put Christmas lights out on the roof all by herself. Of course, she didn't realize they were indoor lights, so they didn't work half the time.

She bought an enormous frozen turkey, but then she forgot it in the trunk of the car and didn't find it until a week later. Needless to say, they were going to have TV dinners on Christmas Day.

Then she decided that she and the girls would go cut down their own Christmas tree. This is the kind of activity that always sounds better in your imagination than it is in reality. After a long walk in the woods, the girls were cold and whiny by the time they found a tree. Annie had brought a little hatchet instead of a saw, and the blade was dull, so it took her about an hour to chop the thing down.

Still, they hauled the tree home and dragged it into the house. Their dog Max took an instant dislike to the tree, growling at it when Annie brought it in the front door. But they set it up and decorated it, and it actually looked pretty good.

The next day, Annie noticed that the tree had a funny smell about it. She didn't pay much attention, but with each passing day, the smell seemed to be getting worse.

On Christmas Eve, Annie put the girls to bed and began to feel pretty blue about the whole Christmas season. To cheer herself up, she tucked all the girls' presents under the tree, put on her bright red flannel robe, and she even put on her Santa hat. She stuck a Christmas CD in the stereo and went to make herself some hot chocolate.

Meanwhile, Max was lying on the rug in front of the fireplace, staring at the Christmas tree. He was mad at Annie. He couldn't figure out why she had brought this thing into the house when it had clearly been marked by some other animal. In dog terms, this was a grave insult, and he was not happy about it. He had tried several times to erase the smell, using the only method known to dogs, but it was still there.

Annie came back from the kitchen just as Max was marking the tree one more time. That was the acorn that broke the reindeer's back, so to speak. She cried for a minute, then she got mad. She was mad at Christmas, mad at the dog, mad at God, even. But most of all, she was mad at the Christmas tree, which represented the whole blinking light, rotten turkey, dog-peed mess.

She threw open the front door, picked up the tree, and just as she was wrestling it out the door, she heard a little voice behind her say, "Santa, why are you taking our Christmas tree?"

That stopped her for a moment. She stood there, trying to decide what to say. That's when she saw the choir across the street, lined up to have their picture taken by a photographer. Behind them, on the roof of the inn, was a naked man, climbing into a bedroom window.

The photographer's flash went off, lighting up the beaming faces of the carolers, as well as the last part of the man to go through the window. The photo appeared in the paper the next day with the caption "Full Moon over Frost Heaves."

All this happened in about two seconds as Annie was standing there trying to think what to tell her daughter. Then she saw a police car pull up in front of the house.

When you have a loved one in the service, the last thing you want to see is a police car pull up in front of your house, especially on Christmas Eve. And the last person you want to see getting out of that police car is a soldier in uniform. Unless, of course, that soldier is the husband you haven't seen in 18 months.

Up at the church, Pastor Woodstead was putting the finishing touches on his sermon when he heard a scream come from down the street. It startled him for a moment, then he realized it was Annie and that she was screaming for joy. He had known that Henry was coming home to surprise Annie for Christmas. Everyone in town knew it, but they hadn't let on. These are Yankees after all, they can keep a secret.

It occurred to Pastor Woodstead that he might be able to work this into his sermon somehow. When he was done, the final paragraph of the sermon looked like this:

You can plan the perfect Christmas, the perfect life, even. Then it all falls apart. And that's when God shows up, usually in a way you never would have expected. So keep your eyes open.

NEWS NUGGETS:
Close call at New Years

There was an excellent turnout for the annual log drop at the town hall on New Year's Eve. With ten seconds left in the old year, the crowd began counting down. At the stroke of midnight, Fred Kimball dropped a nice maple log from the roof of the town hall.

Unfortunately, Fred forgot to look before he let go of the log. As it happens, Millard Tuttle was returning home from the Peabody Inn, where he'd been having a couple of celebratory toots. Millard heard the countdown and stopped right in front of the town hall to see what was happening. Normally, people cheer real loud when the log drops. But this year, everyone was dead silent, which meant they all heard what Millard said when the log missed his head by about two inches. He rang in the New Year with a string of profanity that will go down in the record books for creativity, variety, and delivery. On the plus side, he got to keep the log, and he says it burned real nice.

Millard Takes a Load Off

It has been a long, cold winter in Frost Heaves. The good news is that we were able to hold a winter carnival this year. Once again, Mavis Thompkins sang the opening number, the Star-Spangled Banner. Last year, there was a problem with the fishing derby, which began right after Mavis sang. There were no fish. We can't say for positive that it was Mavis's fault, but we're pretty sure. Anyway, to prevent a similar situation this year, we gave Mavis a microphone, but we didn't actually turn it on. Also, we set up a 10-foot safety buffer around Mavis and no one else was allowed inside it. She was kind of Ground Zero, as it were. As a result, the rest of the carnival went off without a hitch, mostly.

We had the usual events, the free-for-all sliding contest, snow sculptures, and a bonfire. Millard Tuttle won the sliding contest, riding his Pabst Blue Ribbon beer cooler down the hill. Some folks complained because Millard hadn't actually entered the contest, he just fell into the cooler as he reached for his last beer. The rest, as they say, was gravity.

We added a new event this year, a winter triathlon, which consisted of three parts: shoveling a 10 by 20 driveway, then tossing a cord of wood from one pile to another, then thawing out a frozen pipe. After that, the participants had to clear the end of the driveway again because the state plow came by and undid their work. I guess that makes it a quadrathlon.

Once again, the synchronized snowblowers—known as the Snow Men—did a routine out on the town pond. They were led by Ed Whittle, who took over for the late Vern Mullens, in a performance designed to honor Esther Williams, a version of her swim routine from the old movie *Bathing Beauty*—which sounds like a good idea, but it turns out that watching a bunch of old guys in snowmobile suits do a routine isn't nearly as interesting as watching young woman in bathing suits do the same routine. On the plus side, they did get the pond cleared for skating.

As part of the winter carnival festivities, we held a limerick contest. The judges were unanimous in awarding first prize to Herb Cullen for his entry:

There was a bean-eater named Steve,
who sat at the diner each eve,
consuming legumes
and emitting such fumes,
that when he left, all were relieved.

Finally, they showed a movie at the grange hall in the evening. The original plan was to show that movie *Frozen*, but a group of young mothers got up a petition against it. Apparently, if they had to hear that song—you know the one I mean—one more time, someone was going to get hurt. So instead, we showed *Ice Age* for the kids and that

Russian movie, *Dr. Zhivago*, for the adults. Maybe not the best choices, given how cold it has been this winter.

It has been especially cold at the Frost Heaves Community Church—I'm not talking about the people, although they can be a bit standoffish till they get to know you; after 20 years or so, they do tend to warm up. No, I'm talking about the temperature. That old church building is hard to heat, and the furnace has been on its last legs since party lines went out of style. The furnace just can't keep up with the cold we've had, and it got to the point where Pastor Woodstead told folks to bring blankets to church to wrap around themselves. One person, who shall remain nameless—oh, what the heck, it was Barb Whittle—showed up in one of them head-to-toe blankets with arms. She has basically spent the entire winter in that thing, so she figured why change just to go to church?

The winter has been especially long for Pastor Woodstead. Every Sunday, he has had to face his congregation and offer a message of hope and comfort to people who look at him as if he's somehow to blame for the snow piled up to the eaves, the wind blowing through the chinks in the chimney, the frozen pipes, and the ice dams on the roof. I guess they figure he's supposed to have a direct connection to the one in charge of the weather.

Besides being responsible for the weather, Pastor Woodstead finds himself carrying all the burdens of his congregation—the illnesses, the family problems, the financial stresses. After a long winter, those burdens can get pretty heavy.

That's probably why Pastor Woodstead has been spending a lot of time staring out the big old windows of his office, trying to come up with a message of hope and inspiration for his people. The office is on the second floor of the church, looking out over the town, which gives him a bird's-eye view of everything that's going on in Frost Heaves.

When Pastor Woodstead isn't working on his sermon, he tends to daydream about Florida and Arizona, places with golf courses and palm trees, where there's no snow, or cars that won't start, or windshields to scrape. (Believe it or not, there are places where you don't have to worry that you're taking your life in your hands driving to work between the months of November and March, where you don't have to take Dramamine or feel like you're on a slalom course because of the frost heaves.)

Pastor Woodstead is a few years away from retiring, but he has already started clearing out stuff in anticipation. He found a box of old gospel records that belonged to his folks—Tennessee Ernie Ford, George Beverly Shea, and the like. His father used to play them every Sunday morning to get him out of bed for church. Of course, when you are a teenager and your fondest wish is just to sleep in, hearing "When the Roll is Called up Yonder" blaring away on the old RCA Victor is a shock to the system. Only later did he come to appreciate those records.

He held on to those records after his folks died, but they hadn't been played for years, and he decided it was time to get rid of them. He boxed them up and dropped them off at the swap shop at the dump, which is where old technologies go to die: record players, VCRs, 8-track tape decks, cassettes, CD players, and so on.

But as soon as Pastor Woodstead dropped off those records, he began to have second thoughts. When he was a teenager, the last thing he wanted to be was a minister. But music has a way of seeping into you, and over the years, maybe those old gospel songs had had more of an impact than he'd thought.

He went back to the swap shop, but it was too late, the records were already gone. In Frost Heaves, dropping stuff off at the swap shop is like tossing a fish into a room full of cats, it don't last long.

So now Pastor was staring out his office window, thinking about those records, and about Florida, and other things. Then he happened to see Millard Tuttle drive by in his old Chevy pickup with a load of rocks in the back.

Millard was headed to Upper Frost Heaves. I told you about Upper Frost Heaves, the part of town where the few people with any money live, in the only really nice houses. Last year, a fellow from away had bought a pasture there and wanted to build one of them McMansions on it, so he hired Millard to clear the rocks. Hiring Millard was maybe not the smartest move anyone ever made, but as I say, this fella' was from away.

Millard charged a decent price to clear the field and haul the rocks away, dumping them in a big pile in back of his house, waiting for whatever use he might find to put them to. (He's a real Yankee, he don't throw nothing away.)

A year later, the same guy called Millard and asked if he knew of anyone who could build him a stone wall in front of his new house. Millard said he could do it, and he knew where to get a load of prime-quality wall-building stones at a good price. That made the homeowner happy. He thought he was getting a bargain and gave Millard a check to buy the rocks.

You probably know where this story is going. Millard loaded the rocks from his backyard back into the truck and headed off to deliver them. But on the way, he decided to stop off at the Peabody tavern for a celebratory drink and maybe entertain his friends with a story of how he'd pulled one over on the guy from away.

If you know Millard, it won't surprise you that one drink is rarely celebratory enough. By the time he left the tavern, it was dark and snowing pretty hard—too late to deliver the rocks, so he just headed for home. But given the snow, the darkness, and his liquified condition, Millard got lost and eventually found himself in the middle of a large parking lot. He drove around the lot for quite a while but couldn't find an exit, so eventually he decided to just park the truck and wait out the storm. Then he fell asleep.

Luckily for Millard, it was one of the few warm nights we have had. Also, he had a fair bit of 40-proof antifreeze in him, so he was fine.

Millard woke in the morning to a sharp crack like a rifle going off. He snapped awake, looked around, and realized he was sitting in the middle of the town pond, which he had mistaken for a parking lot. The crack he'd heard was the ice on the pond expressing doubt about how much longer it would be able to hold the truck with all those rocks, not to mention Millard.

He started the truck up, but he hadn't moved more than a few inches when the ice reiterated its position on the matter with another series of loud cracks. So Millard turned the truck off and sat there for quite a while, pondering the situation.

After a bit, he noticed that a group of people had gathered at the town beach at the edge of the pond, maybe 100 yards from where the truck was parked. These folks appeared to be talking with each other, scratching their heads, and pointing at the truck. Then he noticed that money was changing hands, and one person was making notes in a notebook. I've already mentioned that whenever we have financial problems in New Hampshire, some genius decides we need to bring in big gambling interests to take our money from us. But we don't need outsiders to do that, we can do it on our own, informal like, and keep the money right here in the state. That's what was going on at the town beach that morning.

Millard was none too happy about this situation, but he had more pressing things on his mind, like trying to think of a way out of this predicament. And as pondered this, he began to hear what sounded like singing coming from the town dump, wafting over the ice from the far side of the pond, behind a hedge of pine trees. And it sounded for all the world as if someone was singing an old gospel tune, in a deep baritone voice.

"Sometimes my path seems drear, without a ray of cheer,

and then a cloud of doubt may hide the light of day.

The mists of sin may rise and hide the starry skies,

but just a little talk with Jesus clears the way."

It turns out Leo LaFleur, who runs the dump, had rescued Pastor Woodstead's old albums and was playing them over the loudspeaker system at the dump on a record player he had also snagged.

Millard Tuttle is not a particularly religious person, but hearing that song, he had a feeling it was a message that Jesus wanted to have a little talk with him. And the gist of the conversation was that Jesus wasn't too pleased with the idea of selling a man's own rocks back to him. Millard thought about arguing the point, but he figured he was on shaky ground, or shaky ice as the case may be.

So, he got out and started to carry the rocks, one by one, away from the truck and set 'em out on the ice. This took quite a while, but as he got rid of those rocks, he felt a weight lift off his soul, not to mention off his rear axle, which was maybe more important at the moment.

Along the shore, the folks watching all this were flummoxed. Some of them wanted to change their bets, others said no, it was too late. Up in his office, Pastor Woodstead was still staring out the window, still trying to come up with a sermon idea. Then he saw Millard unloading those rocks, and it occurred to him that life often loads us down with burdens. And from there, the sermon just started to flow from his pen:

Some burdens are caused by things we carry around with us, things God never intended us to carry. Sometimes we carry other people's burdens. And sometimes the burden gets so heavy we think we're going to crack under the strain.

There is a time to carry those burdens, as Solomon said, a time to weep and a time to laugh, a time to mourn and a time to dance, a time to gather stones and a time to scatter them.

To everything there is a season. Sometimes the season is winter. But winter does come to an end, and then it's time to lay down your burdens, take a deep breath, and cast your cares upon the Lord, because the Lord cares for you.

So there was his sermon. He kept writing, and as he did, for some reason, he found himself humming one of those old songs his father used to play all the time.

"When you feel a little prayer wheel turning
and you will know a little fire is burning
you will find a little talk with Jesus makes it right."

NEWS NUGGETS:
Plows beat Mailboxes

In the annual face-off between the state plows and the local mailboxes, the mailboxes took another beating, as the plows clobbered them 15-0. Local residents, who have tried for years to build plow-proof mailboxes, remain undaunted. "There's always next year," says Fred Kimball.

SPRING

A Leak of His Own

The weather has finally started to warm up in town, and Earl Hadley decided it was time to clean out his pellet stove. You have to do this every once in a while and Earl always puts it off as late as he can.

He hauled out the vacuum and was kneeling in front of the stove, sucking out the soot, when everything started to go dark on him. He panicked, thinking maybe this was the big one, and began to wish he had voted for that portable defibrillator at town meeting after all.

"Vera!" he gasped. "Vera!"

His wife came running to the living room and stopped, staring around the room. There was a layer of black soot all over everything—the furniture, the books, and even over Earl and his glasses.

"You idiot," Vera said. "You've got to put a bag in the vacuum cleaner before you use it."

Earl breathed a deep sigh of relief. "Oh, thank goodness. I thought I was dying."

"You ain't out of the woods yet," she said.

Meanwhile, our postmaster Ed Whittle had a leaky pipe in his cellar last week. He found it when Audrey sent him down to bring up her seed starter trays. It wasn't a bad leak, just a slow drip from a pipe that had caused a pancake-sized puddle on the cellar floor.

Ed could have ignored it. He should have ignored it. But he'd had a bad week at the post office. The computers were causing problems, his people were out sick, and folks were complaining about long waits at the counter, which wouldn't be so long if people didn't have to tell Ed about their hip surgery—the complete, unabridged version— while other folks were waiting.

At any rate, Ed needed something easy to fix so as to boost his self-esteem. And as I say, the leak didn't look that bad. He figured a little duct tape would do the trick.

Ed rooted around his workbench till he found the duct tape, dried off the dripping pipe with a rag, and wrapped a long piece of tape around it several times. When he was finished, the pipe looked like a sore knee with an ace bandage wrapped around it, but the dripping had stopped and Ed was pretty proud of himself.

An hour or so later, Ed went back to the cellar looking for a picture hook so he could hang a new picture Audrey had bought. He was poking around in a tin can full of nails, screws, and fasteners when he heard a sound.

Drip.

Sure enough, the water had worked its way around the duct tape and was dripping at the same rate as before—slow, but steady.

Ed swore under his breath—this was early in the process—and tore off the duct tape. Clearly, this was going to take some serious effort.

He headed out the door and Audrey asked, "Where are you going?"

"Hardware store. Gotta get some stuff to fix a pipe."

Audrey hesitated. In the world of matrimonial affairs, situations like this required the diplomacy of an Adlai Stevenson. "Do you know how to do that?"

Ed snorted. Though he'd never actually done any plumbing, he had helped his brother once, handing Henry supplies as he did the plumbing in the basement of a cabin he'd built himself. So the honest answer to the question was no.

Of course," he said.

A half hour later, Ed came back from Dingle's hardware store with the Handi-Man Plumbing Kit, which included a blowtorch, spark lighter, solder, flux, and do-it-yourself instructions. These days, there are easier ways to fix a leaky pipe, but they're also more expensive, and Ed is cheap.

He spread the parts on his workbench and unfolded the instructions, which were printed in 4-point type. His glasses were upstairs and retrieving them would put him in Audrey's line of fire again, so he decided he didn't need the instructions anyway.

He lit the torch and unwound the solder, held a three-inch piece over the leaky pipe, and aimed the torch at it. The solder melted almost instantly, dripping onto the pipe. He covered the pipe with what looked like a sufficient layer of solder, then stood back to admire his work.

Drip.

He cursed under his breath. Clearly, he needed more solder. He lit the torch again and melted more solder onto the pipe. The solder mounded on the pipe like silver bird droppings and dripped off the sides onto the floor.

"How's it going?" Audrey hollered from the top of the stairs.

"Fine. Just needs a little more solder."

"OK," said Audrey, who had only a vague idea what solder was.

"There," Ed said. He had used about half his solder and achieved the Ace bandage effect again, but this time it was a solid silver bandage. Let *that* try leaking.

He gathered his tools, contemplating how good it felt to work with your hands. It gave one a sense of accomplishment that you just didn't get in the postal game.

He fitted the parts of the soldering kit back into the molded carrying case. Flush with success, he decided to turn over a new leaf when it came to organizing his workbench. From now on, everything would have its own place. He would return tools to their proper spot the minute he finished a project. And he planned to do more projects like this. He needed this kind of work to balance...

Drip.

This time Ed swore loudly, a category three blast of profanity with sustained high winds.

Audrey came to the head of the stairs again. "Are you all right?"

"I'm fine." He took a deep breath. "This is just trickier than I thought."

"Should we call a plumber?"

"*What?*" He couldn't believe it. His own wife didn't think he could complete a project as simple as fixing a leaky pipe. What was she going to suggest next, that they bring in someone to cut their meat for them at dinner time? Maybe someone to brush their teeth? "I can handle it."

"All right," she said. It's amazing how much doubt and sarcasm a woman can squeeze into a simple phrase like, "All right."

I'll move things along here by saying that Ed could not handle it. Two days, several trips to the hardware store, and a hundred dollars in miscellaneous parts later, Ed still had a drip. So he gritted his teeth and called Jasper Bevins at Bevins Plumbing and Heating.

Ed picked Jasper because Jasper is a talker. He has a story to go with every repair job, and he always likes to tell the extended-edition, director's cut version, not the Reader's Digest condensed version. Sometimes folks hesitate to call Jasper because they don't know if they have enough time to listen to his stories that day. But Jasper's a very friendly guy. You'd have to be, I guess, to put up with the nonsense he deals with, having to crawl around dark, dank places, fixing pipes that date back to Ben Franklin's time.

Jasper arrived at Ed's and surveyed the scene: the mounds of solder on the stubborn pipe and the floor below it, silver splatters everywhere, wads of duct tape and tools scattered around. "Had a little trouble, huh?"

"Yeah," Ed said, not meeting Jasper's eyes.

Jasper shut the water off and cut out the offending section of pipe. He replaced it with a new section and two high-tech connectors that didn't need solder, a blowtorch, or expletives. The entire operation took two minutes.

Jasper packed up his stuff and was about to leave when Ed said, "Where are you going?" He had been counting on a good thirty or forty minutes of Jasper's stories.

"I'm all done," Jasper said. "Besides, I gotta go to Millie Tuttle's. Millard broke the kitchen sink and she can't do anything till I get there."

"Well, you're not done here."

Jasper looked around. "What did I miss?"

"Nothing. But you're not done."

Ed explained that he had been trying to fix the leak for two days. He had listened to his wife tell him he couldn't do it about three hundred times. "So here's the deal," he said. "You're going to sit here for an hour and make noises every once in a while. I'll pay you for your time. If you throw in a curse every now and then, I'll give you a bonus."

As it turns out, Jasper Bevins is a pretty good cusser. The job ended up costing Ed three times what it would have without the extra service.

But it was worth it.

Police Log:
Udder Nonsense

On Tuesday, Homer Andrews called Chief Andrews to report that his cow Henrietta had broken a fence and wandered off. Chief Spaulding declined to issue a missing bovine report, telling Homer, "She'll come back. She always does." The cow was later located on Old Scoopnagle Road, where it had become trapped in the mud and was blocking traffic, such as it is. Chief Spaulding called on the fire department, whose members stood around for some time deciding what to do. After rejecting several suggestions, they ended up wrapping a firehose around Henrietta and pulling her out with the truck. The cow seemed none the worse for wear, and the incident was filed in the department's call log under the category "Udder complaints."

Edith on the Case

The way some people deal with a long winter is just to escape it. Doreen Bundworth—her husband Bundy owns the garage in town—decided they needed to go to Florida for two weeks.

Bundy is the kind of guy who doesn't do well on vacations. If he don't have a timing belt to fix or a set of brakes to adjust, he don't know what to do with himself. So when Doreen come up with the Florida idea, Bundy said, "What about Duke?" Duke is their dog, an old black lab.

"Arthur can take care of him," she said.

Arthur Bascom works for Bundy and has done forever. Arthur is a good guy, but not exactly an MIT graduate, if you know what I mean. It was hard enough for Bundy to take time off and leave his garage in Arthur's hands, let alone his dog.

So Bundy kept putting Doreen off. But every time it snowed—and it snowed a lot—Doreen's mood got darker and darker, and Bundy finally realized he was going to have a situation on his hands if he didn't agree to this vacation idea.

"All right, then," he told Doreen. "I guess we can go."

Right away, Doreen started to perk up, and she put together a plan for a weeklong cruise ending up in Florida, followed by a week at an adult community. She asked Edith Wyer—who lives next door—to keep an eye on their house while they were away, which probably wasn't necessary. In Frost Heaves, asking Edith to keep an eye on things is like asking the NSA to monitor your activities—she's already got it well in hand.

"Don't worry," Edith said. "I'll keep an eye out," and Doreen knew she would.

So Doreen and Bundy took off for Florida and Arthur moved into the house. Edith kept a close lookout from her sentry post next door, and for the first few days, everything seemed to go fine, which was kind of disappointing to her. She was hoping to have something to report to Doreen and Bundy when they got back—wild parties, late-night shenanigans, or some other flagrant violation of the social contract.

But Arthur and Duke were getting along just fine. In fact, Duke liked having Arthur around. To begin with, Arthur didn't mind if Duke slept on the bed with him, something Doreen would never tolerate. And for an old dog, the smell of an old guy is more agreeable than flowery soap and shampoo that just masks the good, earthy smell.

After a few days, Arthur ran out of dog food, so he stopped at the market on the way to work and picked up a case of Meaty Meal, Duke's favorite brand. He tossed it in the back of his truck and went off to work, not thinking about what might happen to it there. (Not thinking is one of Arthur's specialties.)

As it happens, a cold snap passed through town that day, as if winter was saying, "I ain't through yet, you know." At any rate, by the end of the day, when Arthur finished work and carried that dog food into the house, it was frozen solid. Bundy has a woodstove, so Arthur set the case of dog food on top of the stove to thaw out and found a couple of leftover hamburgers and some cheese for Duke to eat in the meantime, which suited Duke just fine.

Arthur was feeling hungry himself and decided to walk to town and have a burger and a beer with the guys at the tavern. He ended up having a couple of beers and before he knew it, two hours had passed.

By the time he headed home, the temperature had dropped precipitously and Arthur realized he had made a mistake and was going to be frozen solid by the time he walked back to Bundy's place. He stopped in at the market to warm up and ran into Chief Spaulding.

The chief looked at Arthur doubtfully and shook his head at the thin jacket Arthur was wearing. "You walking?" he asked.

"Yep," Arthur said, kind of sheepish.

"Hang on," the Chief said. "Let me get my coffee and I'll give you a lift."

At just about that time, Edith Wyer was talking to one of her news sources on the phone, getting an update about the marital problems of a couple that shall remain nameless. In the middle of this, she heard what sounded like a gunshot from next door. "I've got to go," she said and hung up quick. (When you are a small-town reporter, you have a responsibility to be there on the spot when news is happening.)

As Edith ran to the window, there was another gunshot, followed by a couple more. She crouched by her window, worried that some of the stray bullets might find their way over to her house. But she wasn't going to miss this, the most exciting true-crime episode to happen in Frost Heaves in years. There was another string of gunshots, then silence. Absolute silence.

Good Lord, Edith thought. *He's dead.* She waited to see if anyone ran out of the house, but no one did. That made her think it must be a case of suicide, but she couldn't figure why it had taken so many shots to finish the job— she had counted an even dozen gunshots, and it was hard to believe even Arthur Bascom was that bad a shot.

She was sorely tempted to go over there so she could file a first-hand report on this murder-suicide-whatever tragedy, but even a dedicated reporter like Edith has her limits. She decided it would be safer to call Chief Spaulding and picked up the phone. But before she could dial, the Chief pulled into the Bundworth's driveway.

"Darn it," she muttered. Someone had beaten her to the punch, which ticked her off more than a little, given that she was right next door.

To her surprise, though, Chief Spaulding didn't even get out of the car. He just pulled up, the passenger door opened, and Arthur Bascom got out. Normally, Edith would not be surprised to see Arthur Bascom being escorted home by the police. But it was a bit shocking to see him up and about, given that he was supposed to be dead.

The Chief drove off and Edith peered out the window, her mouth open, as Arthur stumbled into the house.

Inside the house, Arthur found a scene of devastation, busted-open cans lying strewn about and dog food everywhere. After a moment, he figured out what had happened. That entire case of dog food had thawed out, heated up, and then exploded, spraying Meaty Meal all over the living room like a paint sprayer.

Arthur stood there surveying the scene and Duke came skulking out of the bedroom. He had flown out of the room and hidden under the bed when the shooting began, but he decided it was safe to return now. He padded into the room, looked around, and decided he had died and gone to doggy heaven—a whole room that smelled like Meaty Meal. He looked up at Arthur with what can only be called adoration. As far as he was concerned, Arthur was a god, or at the very least, the best person on the planet.

Arthur got a mop and began cleaning up. A good part of the Meaty Meal eruption had hit the ceiling, the rest of it landed on the wood floor, which Duke helped clean up with his tongue. Then he gave Bundy's leather recliner the once-over and a slick, dog-spit finish.

It took a day or two, but Arthur had pretty much cleaned up the place by the time Doreen and Bundy got home. They never did find out what happened. Edith couldn't tell them because she never knew exactly what went on. She had tried to pry the story out of Arthur, but he wasn't about to tell her. His reputation as a doofus didn't need embellishing and besides, he is a real Yankee. He can make a clam seem downright chatty.

154

Anyway, Doreen and Bundy were glad to be back. The trip was a disaster—that's another story I'll tell you sometime, but let's just say they were happy to be home again.

As they got into bed that night, Bundy said to Doreen, "Did you feed the dog?"

"Yes. What makes you ask that?"

"I don't know," he said. "Something just made me think of dog food."

NEWS NUGGETS:
New business in town

Herb Cullen has announced the opening of a new addition to his farmstand, which he is calling Herb's Herbs. "I got the idea from this fancy place that sells herbs and puts on gourmet lunches," he says. His wife loves that place, and he decided he could do the same thing. For spices, Herb plans to offer the usual stuff, like parsley, sage, rosemary, and chives. "A lot of chives," he says. And while he can't offer gourmet lunches, he promises that, "The missus makes a pretty good tuna noodle casserole."

Muck Ado About Nothing

We held another meeting of the FRED council last week and Edith Wyer came up with an idea for a fundraiser. "You know how some places have spelling bees?" she said.

Right away, the rest of us got nervous because any idea that depends on the intellectual capacity of the people of Frost Heaves, young or old, has about as much chance of success as a fish on snowshoes, maybe less.

But what Edith had in mind was a gossip bee. People would sign up as teams and the judge—that would be Edith—would throw questions at 'em about local gossip. (Edith herself would not be on a team, because that would be like competing against Jesus in a breadmaking contest. The average person wouldn't stand a chance.)

At first, we all thought the gossip bee sounded like a good idea. Then Edith started rattling off some sample bits of gossip, several of which landed a little too close to home. Let's just say the gossip bee idea has been tabled indefinitely.

Besides, we're busy getting ready for the next big event in town, Mud Week. Folks in New England who like to complain—and frankly, that's a large percentage of the population—are fond of saying that we only have two seasons: nine months of winter and three months of darn poor sledding. But that's not entirely true. Our New England summers are glorious, and autumn is so beautiful that people come from all over just to stare at our trees. Even winter is great if you're into outdoor activities like hurtling down a snow-covered mountain on a pair of slippery wooden sticks.

But spring in New England is a hard sell, especially the early part of spring when it's cold, damp, and still mostly gray. The outstanding feature of early spring in New England is mud—miles and miles of dirt roads that turn into thick sludge thanks to the spring rains and snow melt.

Of course, for some of the men in Frost Heaves, mud season is a major sporting event. Don't ask me why a guy who spends hours making sure his truck is sparkly clean can't wait to get out on a dirt road and see how much mud he can kick up. Getting stuck in the mud? That's like winning some sort of prize.

Mud season provides surefire entertainment for locals as they watch people from away drive luxury cars on roads that anyone with the common sense of a turnip would think twice about. "It's drama, comedy, and suspense all at once," says Homer Cratchet, who admits that his TV hasn't worked in quite a while.

A few years back, the FRED council was trying to think of a way to promote springtime as a reason for people to visit Frost Heaves, some kind of tourist draw along the lines of foliage season. After kicking around a bunch of ideas, we came up with Mud Week, a week of mud-related activities for the whole family.

The main event of Mud Week is always the Muddy Roads Rally, which follows a tortuous route along some of our least negotiable thoroughfares. Entrants receive extra points if they locate any of the previous year's participants, a few of whom were never seen again after leaving the starting line.

Another popular event is the Mud Sculpture contest, which is like those sand sculpture contests at the beach, except you don't need sunscreen. The contest draws artists from as far away as East Mildew, and visitors enjoy watching them at work, folks like Lloyd "Mudhen" Fletcher, whose winning entry last year—a replica of the Mayflower—was described as "quite moving" —especially after the rain started.

Mount Fillmore, our local ski area, gets in on the action when the last of the snow is gone. "We haul out the mud skis, mud boards, and mudboggans," says manager Irene Muchmore. This year, Irene promises 6 to 12 inches of finely groomed mud on all trails, including the notorious black diamond "Washboard Alley."

For the less adventurous, Herb Cullen has come up with a new sport called mud-shoeing. Strap on a pair of Herb's mudshoes (which look an awful lot like old snowshoes) and follow Herb on a hike through the area's most scenic slush. Herb has also ordered a line of biodegradable mud boots from Wanderers Supply. "If you get stuck, just step out of them," Herb says. "By summer, they'll be mulch."

Another exciting activity we've planned this year is Senior Mud Wrestling. Visitors will cheer on the octogenarians of Frost Heaves as they strip down and tangle in the topsoil for coveted prizes such as visits from their children. Note, this activity is not for the faint of heart—the people watching, that is.

On the cultural front, the Frost Heaves Historical Society will present a special exhibit, "Mud Through the Ages," with such exciting and educational exhibits as Hiram Bostner's "Old Faithful" tow chain, which pulled 1037 cars and trucks from the mud before it snapped a link and was retired. There's also an innovative "mud shovel," a variation on the snow shovel that never really caught on. The exhibit is guaranteed to be minutes of fun for the whole family.

Up at the town hall, you won't want to miss our local dance troupe, the Frost Heaves High Steppers, doing an original composition in honor of Mud Week called "Stuck!" It's kind of like River Dance only slower, especially if we get a late freeze.

Local residents have come up with a new party game that's all the rage at Mud Week parties. It's called Bobbing for Boots. Participants stick their arms into a tub of mud to see what they can pull out: a pair of shoes, hiking boots, hubcaps—you never know!

The finest eateries in Frost Heaves—also the not-so-fine and the take-your-chances places—will offer a variety of mud-themed meals and specialties. Stop by the Bluebell Diner to sample their mudloaf—meatloaf fortified with oat bran, so thick you won't be able to get your fork out of it. Top that off with Muddy Road ice cream (basically Rocky Road that's melted), or a Café Mudchiato—a hearty blend of coffee aged to perfection on the back burner for several days and blended with just enough cream and sugar to remove it from the Toxic Substances Control list.

Up to the tavern at the Peabody Inn, Elwood Peabody has invented a new drink in honor of mud season. He mixes coffee liqueur with a little cider vinegar, and just as he serves it to you, he drops in an Alka Seltzer tablet. He calls it Mud in Your Eye. It's quite dramatic.

Ladies, why pay top dollar for a mud facial at some fancy-schmancy spa? Stop by Homer Andrews' farm for a bargain-basement beauty treatment that will leave your skin as clean and refreshed as those high-class treatments without emptying your pocketbook. Homer uses only organic, free-range mud, enriched by contributions from the livestock on his own farm.

So that's the lineup for this year's Mud Week. We have been trying to convince the Eldercoach Bus Lines to get involved with a Mud Peeper's tour of some of our muddiest main streets and back roads. We even thought of a clever name for the tour: Sedimental Journeys. So far, we haven't been able to drum up much interest from them, I don't know why.

NEWS NUGGETS:
Swap Shop Registry

In honor of spring weddings coming up, the folks at the swap shop have set up a gift registry, just like the big box stores like Bed, Bath, and Beyoncé. Couples looking for a perfectly good toaster or a complete set of almost matching cups and saucers should get their names on the list ASAP.

In the Cards

The big excitement around Frost Heaves lately has
been the final game of the bingo season, the lead-up
to the regional championships.

Verna Depres is the local champ, a regular Minnesota
Fats of bingo. Verna's not from around here, originally.
She was born and raised in Manchester, in one of the
French neighborhoods where they sell beignets at the
corner market and folks have pictures of Jesus over their
beds. She spent thirty years working at the Elm City shoe
factory, back when shoes were still made in this country.
After her husband Frank died, she moved to Frost Heaves
to be near her daughter Alice, but then Alice moved to
Palm Beach a year later, which should tell you something
about that relationship.

After Alice left, Verna adopted a new family: Bingo.
She became a regular on the bingo circuit: the Legion Hall
in East Mildew on Thursday nights, St. Gertrude's in
Milliwillitockset on Fridays, mid-week at the town hall in
Crowfly Corners. But every Saturday, Verna is on her
home turf, laying down her cards at the grange building
next door to the Frost Heaves Community Church. The
church actually owns the grange building, which explains a

couple of innovations to the game as it's played in our town.

Technically, being Protestant, the church doesn't hold with bingo (unlike the Catholics, for whom bingo is practically a sacrament). So instead of running the operation itself, the church leases the building to the Ladies Loon League every Saturday night and they do the dirty work. That way, the church isn't directly involved in a sinful enterprise, it's just subletting the sin. Most of the members of the Loon League are also members of the church, which makes it handy.

The church's stake in the business also explains why they call it "beano" instead of "bingo." They use kidney beans instead of chips to mark the cards, and somehow, this is supposed to drain the sin out of the operation. Don't ask me to explain how that works.

Finally, in Frost Heaves, we don't play for money, we play for prizes—a jug of maple syrup, a gift certificate from the Bait 'n' Beauty salon, maybe a new set of snow tires for a really big prize. Again, I don't understand the distinction between cash and prizes, sin-wise, but I'm sure God does.

Bingo is supposed to be a game of luck, with no particular skill involved. But you couldn't tell that by Verna, who has been winning steady ever since she moved to town, and no one knows how she does it. Maybe she just picks cards that have the right numbers, numbers that are more likely to get called. It's a fact that serious bingo sharks get to know the cards and will stand in line waiting to get in as soon as the door opens to claim their special cards.

Other folks, with a more mathematical bent, say it's just a matter of numbers. The more you play, the more likely you are to win. Most of the regulars play four, six, or even eight cards. Verna plays sixteen cards. It takes a quick eye to play that many cards, or else you'll miss a number before the next one is called.

Beyond that, some folks count on their lucky charms to help them—knickknacks, statues of St. Jude, pictures of grandchildren, the occasional four-leaf clover—all lined up and looking over the cards as if they could influence which ball the caller pulls out of the tumbler. (As you can see, despite the church's arm's-length relationship to the whole business, there's a fair bit of faith involved.)

Verna doesn't need charms. Besides being quick and having that wall of cards, she intimidates the other players. Back when smoking was allowed at the games, Verna puffed on an endless chain of Camels that kept a thick cloud around her at all times. These days, she sucks on

___________ mints all night long.* And even those mints are part of her strategy.

Bingo games tend to get quiet towards the end of a round, what with everyone concentrating on their cards. But about that time, Verna will unwrap a mint, crinkling the wrapper real slow. The way Verna does it, it's like the Chinese water torture. The crinkling throws people off their stride and makes them forget what they were doing.

---

* Note to potential advertisers: You know how movies have product placements in them? I can't see why that wouldn't work in books. For the right price, I could put your mints in that space. I'll consider other hard candies and maybe even chocolates, but probably not popcorn. You have to draw the line somewhere.

Folks have been known to miss numbers being called because they were distracted by the crinkling.

Bingo season always starts after Labor Day and ends in the spring, around the time the Burpee catalog arrives and people start fantasizing about Big Boy tomatoes and Golden Beauty corn. The final night of the season is the playoffs, the winner of which goes on to the BingOlympics. This is the Big Show, the Wimbledon of bingo, and includes an all-expenses-paid trip to Portland. That alone—the chance to get out of Frost Heaves in late winter—is reason enough to compete.

The playoff winner always gets a big write-up in the Bingo Gazette ("Your Complete Guide to Bingo in the Northeast") and appearances on all the major media: the Frost Heaves Free Advertiser, the Morning Club with Thelma Delmar on WHAT radio, and New Hampshire Byways, which is on the public access channel out of Milliwillitockset.

Of course, there's also the prestige. People look at you differently after you've been to the bingo championships. They watch you pick your cards to see if they can figure out your secret. They study the way you snap your beans onto the numbers.

With all that attention, it's no surprise that the BingOlympics changes a person. Not that most of us would ever know, since Verna was always the winner. But there was always hope.

The excitement was high the night of the recent playoffs. I showed up early to get a good seat and snag my lucky card. (No, I won't tell you.) I was also wearing my lucky underwear, the pair I had on the night I won the notorious "Upside-Down T" round and got the tickets to see Hank Hamshaw and his Rubber Band play over in Birdley Brook.

Right away, the playoffs promised to be a night to go down in bingo history. It all started when Verna took Louise Mitchell's lucky card. Here's how that went down.

Years ago, Louise stumbled on a bingo card that read 6-1-4-7-5 under the B, which is her wedding anniversary: June 14, 1975. She knew right away that it was a sign—someday she was going to win big playing that card. She had played it every Saturday night for ten years and so far she hadn't won a thing with it, but that didn't bother her. She figured the card was saving up for a really big win. (I told you there was a fair bit of faith involved in this game.)

Technically, of course, picking cards is first-come, first-served. But the regulars know each other's special cards and leave them alone. Except for the night of the playoffs.

Louise was standing next to Verna at the card table and happened to look over as Verna pulled Louise's lucky card out of a box. Verna did it so slyly, slipping it under another card, that Louise almost missed it.

She cleared her throat. "Excuse me, Verna. I think you've got my card."

Verna glared at her as if Louise had accused her of stealing her husband. "What?"

"My card," Louise said, pointing to the stack that Verna was sliding to the far side of her body. "I think that's my lucky card."

"I have no idea what you're talking about," Verna said and carried the cards over to the cashier.

Louise was speechless. This was an unheard-of breach of bingo etiquette. Then she realized what was happening.

It was a tactical move on Verna's part. Louise was Verna's only real competition in the play-off—a serious contender with a quick eye and a steady bean hand—and Verna was trying to psych her out.

Louise was shaken, but she disappeared for a few minutes to the ladies' room in the hallway next to the pay phone. By the time she returned, she had composed herself, and it would have taken thumbscrews to get her to admit anything was wrong. She picked a card at random to complete her set and took a seat as far away from Verna as she could get.

Folks went about their business, setting up their cards and good-luck charms, but you could feel the tension in the air, as if a storm were brewing. Everyone knew what Verna had done, but no one said anything, of course. You don't poke a porcupine, even if it does steal the suet from your bird feeder.

A few minutes later, everyone's attention was distracted by the arrival of a newcomer. We don't get many visitors to Frost Heaves, and a newcomer to bingo night stands out like a cucumber in a pumpkin patch. Especially this newcomer, a woman in bright green stretch pants, a yellow ski jacket, and hair the color of a highway cone. She looked like a road flare going off.

She hung her jacket on a peg by the door. Underneath, she had on a fuzzy white sweater with little spangles all over it. The spangles glittered when she moved, which was constantly—fluffing her hair, jangling her bracelets—and she had more bracelets than one of those rap musicians.

The stranger went to the card table and picked her cards as if she were choosing mums at the florist, with a low, running commentary. "Oh, that one looks good. And that one'll do. Let's see now..."

She paid for her cards and scanned the room for a seat. Being the playoffs, there weren't a lot of empty places, but there was one next to Verna, in the dead center of the room. On Verna's right was her best friend Marguerite LaPlante, who never won and seemed happy enough to bask in the glow of Verna's fame. No one was sitting on Verna's left, not on this night. If you'd put a shrub next to Verna that night, it probably would have wilted.

But the stranger looked around and saw there was nowhere else to sit. "Oh, there's a place," she said and headed for the seat next to Verna.

The room hadn't been so quiet since the time Reverend Woodstead asked for volunteers to put in a new septic system behind the church. A few folks actually gasped.

Of course, everyone felt sorry for the stranger. She had no idea what she was walking into. To begin with, Verna has no patience with irregular bingo players, folks who don't take the sport seriously, and even less with the occasional drop-ins. As far as she's concerned, casual players are like people who only go to church on Christmas and Easter. Also, sitting next to Verna was an honor. It was like plunking yourself down next to Caesar—you didn't do it unless you were asked.

But this woman did. She fell into the seat as if it were a deck chair on an ocean liner, then turned to Verna and said, "Hah there."

Verna stared as if the woman had spoken Greek. "What?"

"I said, hah there." She held out a plump hand.

Verna nodded, ignoring the hand, and mumbled a greeting that only bats and a few species of dogs could have picked up.

"I'm Ahnez Mobley," the woman said. "From Joejah."

"What?"

"Georgia, silly. Mare-yetta, Georgia. I'm here visiting my sister-in-law."

"Mmm," Verna said, turning back to her cards.

Inez Mobley blinked, looked around at the others—who quickly buttoned their gazes back on their own cards—and began to get the picture. "Well heck, I'd better set my cards out."

She tossed her cards down haphazardly, in no particular pattern, and Verna glanced over. The edges weren't even lined up for Pete's sake, and there were five of them.

A murmur rippled through the crowd; the woman was playing five cards. *Five.* It was unheard of. People always played an even number of cards: four, six, eight, or ten. Children sometimes played one card, just to keep them quiet. If you had walking pneumonia and were at death's door, you could get away with three cards, lined up in a neat row in front of you. But that was only a temporary concession, just till the antibiotics kicked in. No one played five cards.

Verna turned back to her own cards, eyebrows raised. She didn't need to say a word. It was as if the newcomer had just farted in church.

Gus Pickering began calling numbers for the first game. Verna didn't like Gus because he tended to mumble, plus his dentures were loose, so you couldn't always tell if he was saying 33 or 13. Occasionally, someone would yell, "Recall" to have him repeat a number, which ticked Verna off because it slowed down the game. She figured if people couldn't keep up they should stay home and watch "Lifestyles of the Rich and Idiotic" on TV.

The first game that night was the Cover-All Jackpot, where if you cover all the numbers on your card with the first 24 balls called, you win all the prizes for the night. The chances of that happening are about 25 quadrillion to one, so after the first 24 numbers, they start taking away prizes until someone wins, usually after 60 or 70 numbers. For the first 24 numbers though, tension is high, since you never know, a person *could* win that big jackpot.

As Gus called the numbers, Inez rattled around in her purse and pulled out a pack of _________ chewing gum.*
She held the pack out to Verna. "Like a piece?"

Verna held up a hand to ward off the gum as if it were radioactive.

"Suit yourself," Inez said, unwrapping a piece and stuffing it into her mouth, accordion style. "You know, we don't play much bingo where I come from. We—"

"Beano," Verna said, hoping to shut her up.

"Excuse me?"

"It's called 'beano.'"

"Oh. I'm sorry, darlin'. That's right, you folks call it beano around here. My sister-in-law says that's 'cause y'all are so full of beans. That's a joke, a' course."

---

* Advertisers, see my previous note.

Gus called, "Under the N, twelve."

Verna turned her attention to Gus as if he were Abe Lincoln giving the Gettysburg Address, hoping Inez would get the message. She didn't.

"Anyway, we don't play bingo," she said. "I'm sorry, there I go again—beano. We play keno. It's real similar, 'cept the numbers go higher and there's no free square in the middle, and it doesn't say anything at the top, not even Keno, course it wouldn't anyways 'cause Keno only has four letters and there are five squares, so that wouldn't work unless you spelled it k,e,a,n,o, which I guess you could, because if there's such a thing as beano, why couldn't you have keano?" She turned to Verna. "Well really, why not?"

Verna stared at her, finally recognizing this woman for who she was: the Anti-Christ. Or at least, the Anti-Yankee.

"Under the O, nine," Gus called.

"Well," Inez said, "it's about time," sliding a bean into place with a red-lacquered fingernail. "I swear, I'm going to trade these cards in if they don't—"

Gus called a number, but Verna couldn't hear it over the chattering.

"Recall!" Verna shouted, with a sharp glance at Inez.

"B-4," Inez whispered to her. "Just like the word 'before.' Isn't that funny?"

Verna deposited a bean on her eighth card and gave Inez a look that would fry bacon, but Inez didn't seem to notice.

The game went on and Verna's number eight card continued to fill up. For the first time, it occurred to her that she might actually have a shot at winning the cover-all jackpot.

"Under the I, twenty-seven," Gus said—another one for Verna's number eight card, and now her heart was racing.

"Why, look at you," Inez said, leaning over towards Verna's cards. "Y'all are moving right along there. How's this work again, you have to cover—"

"Shhh!" Verna hissed at Inez and instantly regretted it. Shushing at bingo was like blowing your horn on Main Street—it generally wasn't necessary and made you look as if you were losing control.

"Under the N, eleven," Gus said.

"I'm sorry," Inez said. "I know you have to concentrate, so I'm just going to pay attention to my own cards now and let you—"

"Under the G, thirty-nine."

It was another bean for Verna's number eight card. Now the presence of Inez Mobley became unbearable. Verna knew how pro golfers must feel when they're trying to concentrate on their shot and some idiot in the gallery has a hacking cough.

"Under the B, twenty-two."

Vern slid another bean onto her number eight card. She was breathing hard now, wishing she could light up a Camel to steady her nerves. The card only had two blank numbers left.

"Good golly," Inez said. "It sure looks like you're about to—"

"Shhhh," Verna said. By this point, she would have shushed Mother Teresa.

"I'm sorry," Inez whispered. "I said I was going to mind my own beeswax and that's what I'm going to do. I'm just going to—"

"Under the I, five."

Verna's hand trembled as she placed a bean onto her number eight card. She'd never heard of anyone actually winning the Cover All Jackpot with just 24 numbers called. She would go down in the Bingo Book of World Records. She'd be in the Bingo Hall of Fame. They'd probably put a plaque on her seat.

Inez unwrapped another piece of gum and wadded up the paper. She put it beside her cards, but it rolled off the table.

Gus called, "Under the G—"

Inez reached down for the paper, moving her chair with a screech that drowned out the number.

"For the love of God," Verna yelled at Inez. "Will you please—"

"Under the O, twenty-six," Gus said.

"Wait," Verna yelled. "I didn't get—"

"Bingo," came a quiet voice from the other side of the room.

It was Louise Mitchell, playing the random card she'd picked up in place of her lucky card.

For two seconds, the hall was silent. Then, pandemonium broke out. Louise began reading her numbers back to Gus to make sure she'd got them right. Verna was yelling about calling the bingo commissioners. Inez was telling Verna how sorry she was, and everyone else was saying, didn't that beat all, who would have thought, and it wasn't even Louise's lucky card, and so on.

Despite Verna's protest, Louise Mitchell is going to the BingOlympics this year. Louise still says she wouldn't have won if not for her lucky card. According to her, that card sacrificed itself so she could pick the winning card. If that's not faith, I don't know what is.

Personally, I think she owes it all to her sister-in-law Inez, who had been cleaning up the supper dishes when Louise called and convinced her to come play bingo. Louise had been looking forward to an evening without Inez's never-ending chatter. But then Verna took Louise's lucky card. Louise and Inez had never gotten along that well, but I think they're going to be good friends from now on. Like I said, being a bingo champion changes you.

NEWS NUGGETS:
Charlie's Spa

Charlie Dingle, over to Dingle's Hardware, has a new side business at his store. "I read how spas were the up-and-coming thing," he says. "That's where ladies go for their nails, waxing, and massages." Charlie has fixed up a room at the back of the store with soft lighting, comfy chairs, candles, and quiet music playing. Out front is a new sign that reads, "Charlie's Spa." For nails, he's got finish nails, drywall nails, and roofing nails. For waxing, he's got floor wax and car wax. "I haven't quite figured out massages," Charlie says, "though I do have a floor buffer that could give you a pretty good workout."

A Wedding, a Baptism, and a Funeral

We held the final meeting of the Frost Heaves Regional Economic Development council this week. We decided the council had completed its mission to boldly go where no committee had gone before, or thought of going if they were as smart as your average bag of wood pellets.

Our goal has always been to put Frost Heaves back on the map, but despite our best efforts—all right, maybe they weren't our best efforts, let's say second-best, or even reheated, leftover efforts—we have failed. Basically, we have expended a lot of time and energy and achieved nothing, and no organization can go on like that forever, except of course the government.

Edith Wyer put forth a motion that we disband the committee, but Walter Dunton suggested that we should just reform the group as a bowling team, which everyone agreed would probably be a better use of our time.

In other news, it was a busy weekend up to the Frost Heaves Community Church, where Pastor Woodstead has also been thinking about moving on. Actually, he has been thinking about retiring for some time now. He is tired, tired of the Snowflake Fair and the ladies arguing about which way the tables should go. Tired of worrying about whether Mavis Thompkins is going to sing another special number that will drive away any newcomers who might have wandered into the church. He's tired of arguing about budgets, committees, agendas, and where the silverware goes in the kitchen. Basically he's just tired, and he doesn't want to go out like the previous pastor, Edwin Twitchell, who literally died in the pulpit. (That's another story for another time.) And if Pastor Woodstead had any doubts that it was getting time to move on, this last weekend just confirmed it for him.

First, there was the wedding on Saturday. The young couple getting married showed up wearing earphones, with which they intended to listen to their own music during the wedding. They hadn't been able to agree on what music to have and that was their solution, one that didn't bode well for the marriage, as far as Pastor Woodstead was concerned.

Still, the ceremony went fine, until Pastor was giving his charge to the couple about the meaning of marriage, when there was a funny buzzing sound outside the church, like someone running a leaf blower, or a small helicopter passing by, which distracted everyone, especially Pastor Woodstead.

Then came the reception at the vestry next to the church. Mabel Pillsbury, she's the Julia Child of Frost Heaves, was in charge of food. By request of the groom, the hors d'oeuvres consisted of beanie weenies—which was his idea of haute cuisine—and Mabel made coleslaw to go with 'em. She was expecting a big crowd, and since she didn't have a bowl large enough to mix it in, she used her bathtub. (Don't worry, she bleaches the tub first, which is probably what gives it that special flavor.)

The reception went all right, although there was the usual problem of the best man and the father of the bride giving speeches. They both thought they were comedians, but they were about as funny as the voice at the station that reads off train stops. Don't you hate it when some guy who thinks he's funny goes on and on, telling long, pointless stories? I sure do.

Anyway, the big excitement at the reception had to do with Agnes Letourneau. Agnes had heard there wasn't going to be a bar at the reception, so she figured it was going to be about as much fun as cleaning lint from the clothes dryer, maybe less. Then she found out there would be a champagne toast. Most folks in Frost Heaves aren't champagne drinkers, so they just took a little sip and left the rest. But Agnes, being a good Yankee, couldn't see letting all that champagne go to waste. When the band started playing and folks got up to dance, she went around and helped herself to all the unwanted champagne on the tables. Let's just say that by the time the band got to the Hokey Pokey, Agnes had become a dancing queen, totally forgetting that several of her major joints had been repaired, replaced, or recalled.

Herb Cullen saw what was happening and came up with a plan. He asked the band to play Love Shack and started a conga line. Agnes got swept up in the line, which danced out of the building and down the sidewalk, where her neighbor Marie had pulled up a car with the passenger door open. Someone shoved Agnes into the car and slammed the door before she knew what was happening and took her home. When Agnes realized how she had been hornswoggled, she was pretty ticked, but fortunately, she don't remember anything about it now.

The next day, Sunday, there was a baptism at the church with some folks who were only occasional attendees. They had invited a lot of relatives for the baptism of the baby, whose name was Allegia, which sounds like some kind of blood pressure medication, don't it? As I say, these were not regular church-goers, so they weren't really with the program. For example, during the offering, when folks are usually quiet—handing over money isn't easy for Yankees, so it's a somber time— these folks talked right through it, as if it were a halftime commercial during the Super Bowl, which they probably would have paid more attention to.

Then, as the actual baptism began, several folks rushed forward to film it with their phones. Pastor Woodhead had already started, so he didn't feel like he could stop, but he really wanted to say, "What on earth do you think you're doing? This is a church, for crying out loud, not an amusement park. This child is entering into a holy contract with God, not going on the spinning-teacups ride."

Then, just as he was pouring the water over the baby's head, that loud buzzing sound came from outside the church again. Pastor Woodstead wanted to say, "Oh, for crying out loud," but instead he said, "I baptize you in the name of the Father, and the Son, and the Holy Spirit," while he still had the chance.

That evening, there was a funeral for Clifford Scraggs, a long-time member of the church. Elmer Cratchet and his wife Edith were there, and during the service Elmer leaned over to Edith and said, "I want you to promise me one thing. When I'm gone, I want you to marry Earl Hadley."

"Earl Hadley?" she said. "You've hated him all your life."

"Ayuh," Elmer said. "Still do." *

Millie and Millard Tuttle were at the funeral, too. On the way out, Millard said to Pastor Woodstead, "Good job. Will you do my funeral?"

"Of course," Pastor said. "When did you want to schedule that?"

"Well, I don't know," Millard said. "The wife would probably like it to be next week."

Millie shrugged and said, "I got nothing going *this* week."

By the end of the day, what with the wedding, the conga line, the baptism, and the funeral, Pastor was exhausted. Also, he hadn't eaten much, since the food after the funeral was mostly leftover beanie weenies and coleslaw. As he was turning out the lights in the church, the room started to swirl, like them old movies when they go into a dream sequence and everything spins out of focus. Then things went dark for a while.

When Pastor opened his eyes, he was lying on the floor, staring up at the ceiling. It reminded him of being a kid in church, when he was bored and would lean his head back against the pew and stare up at the old-fashioned tin tiles overhead. Back then, he had imagined that God lived up there behind the ceiling, and after a while the ceiling

---

* This is an old joke, one you may have heard before. I feel a little bad about reusing it, but not too bad. Shakespeare stole a lot of his material from others, too.

came to represent God—high up, ornate, removed and yet watching over everyone. Now, lying there, he decided that as symbols went, it wasn't a bad image for God, one that people lost when they grew up and were no longer allowed to lean back, rest their heads on the pew, and simply stare up at the ceiling.

He decided he would have to try that sometime during a sermon—have everyone lean back in their seats, rest their heads on the mahogany tops of the pews, and stare up at the ceiling for a period of silent meditation.

Then he heard something he thought might be the fluttering of angel wings, which, given his situation, probably wasn't a good thing. He turned his head to look out the window and saw a funny-looking bird fly by, kind of slow like. He was still thinking about that, wondering if it was an angel, as he closed his eyes and the dark curtain fell.

Pastor was still lying on the floor in the sanctuary when Dottie McPhee came back to the church because she'd left her music there. She called 911 and the ambulance rushed Pastor Woodstead to the hospital. It turned out he was OK, he just had something called tachycardia, which is when the heart is revving but the clutch isn't engaged, so you don't go nowhere.

The doctors put in a pacemaker, and Pastor had to spend a few days in recovery. Lying there in the hospital bed gave him time to think about things, like the fact that sometimes God has to put you on your back to make you slow down. Also, he wondered if that odd sound he kept hearing was in fact an angel or maybe the Holy Spirit hovering around during events that were significant to the folks involved, even if those events hadn't gone all that smoothly.

Other folks in town had heard that strange noise, too. The last person to hear it was Everett Northrup, who lives just outside of town. He was sitting by his window reading the National Perspirer. That's the paper that has headlines like "Kim Kardashian Discovers Cure for Cancer at Stonehenge." Everett heard that buzzing sound and rushed outside. He don't see too well, but he could see well enough to know that it was one of them UFO things he'd been reading about, just hovering over his yard.

Actually, what it was, was a drone sent over by the state. Somebody up to the Concord finally got tired of all the letters and phone calls from the FRED council and decided maybe Frost Heaves should be put back on the map. So they took a break from their important casino promotion efforts and sent a drone out to take pictures and figure out exactly where Frost Heaves was, what roads went through it, and so on.

The drone had just about completed its work when it passed over Everett Northrup's house and hovered there for a bit. The last photo it took was of a wild-eyed man standing in his front yard, aiming an ancient 12-gauge double-barrel shotgun at it. If that drone had been as smart as a pigeon or a wild turkey, it would have taken off, but it wasn't. A few minutes later, what remained of the drone was scattered in pieces all over Everett Northrup's yard, along with whatever chances Frost Heaves ever had of getting back on the map.

I guess that's OK. After all this time, we're used to being ignored, and as Yankees, we don't really mind being left alone.

Well, that's what's been happening in Frost Heaves. As always, I thank you for your attention.

The End

About the Author

Yankee humorist Fred Marple has appeared on stage, screen, and at town halls, church basements, and the homes of most of his friends, usually right around dinner time. Fred is the author of *Welcome to Frost Heaves* and two recordings of original folk songs, *My Mountain* and *Crabby Road*. Fred's video spoof "Yoga for Yankees" has been viewed over 6 million times online. Fred is a graduate of the Frost Heaves Academy and the East Coast School of Knife Sharpening and Carburetor Repair. You can check out all his nonsense online at **fredmarple.com**

Fred bears a striking resemblance to author and humorist Ken Sheldon, a lifelong New Englander who has lived in several small towns that are very close to Frost Heaves. "In fact," he says, "sometimes you can't tell where those towns leave off and Frost Heaves begins." Ken's writings have appeared in *Yankee, The Old Farmer's Almanac, New Hampshire Magazine*, and others. He is the author of novels for children and adults, including the true-crime book *Deep Water—Murder, Scandal, and Intrigue in a New England Town*. Visit him online at **kensheldon.com**. Complaints, dunning letters, and cease and desist orders may be directed to **fred@frostheaves.com**.

[These pages were left blank on purpose. You can use them for phone numbers, your grocery list, or notes from the monthly Loon Lodge meeting. Up to you.]

www.ingramcontent.com/pod-product-compliance
Lightning Source LLC
Chambersburg PA
CBHW031305120726